ABOVE

AND

BEYOND

by Robert C. Hollingsworth

Order this book online at www.trafford.com
or email orders@trafford.com

Most Trafford titles are also available at major online book retailers.

Unless otherwise indicated, Bible quotations are taken from the King James (version) of the Bible.
Names referenced have been used for literary purposes and do not represent actual persons.

Note for Librarians: A cataloguing record for this book is available from Library
and Archives Canada at www.collectionscanada.ca/amicus/index-e.html

Printed in Victoria, BC, Canada.

ISBN: 978-1-4269-1713-4 (sc)
ISBN: 978-1-4269-1714-1 (dj)

Library of Congress Control Number: 2009936632

*Our mission is to efficiently provide the world's finest, most comprehensive book publishing
service, enabling every author to experience success. To find out how to publish your book, your
way, and have it available worldwide, visit us online at www.trafford.com*

Trafford rev. 9/29/09

 www.trafford.com

North America & international
toll-free: 1 888 232 4444 (USA & Canada)
phone: 250 383 6864 ♦ fax: 812 355 4082

Also by Robert C. Hollingsworth

SPRING OF MY LIFE

HYPHENATED – WHY?

~~~~~~~~~~~~~~~~~~~~~~

"Now to Him who is able to do
immeasurably more than all we ask or
imagine, according to His power that is at
work within us".
Ephesians 3:20 (N.I.V.)

~~~~~~~~~~~~~~~~~~~~~~

Contents

Chapter One
RESOLUTION

THE DAY started as it had for Charley for as long as he had been employed and had been working in the office. As he was leaving to start the 30 minute drive to his office, he paused to make sure everything was 'in place' before he set out to meet the public.

Charley prided himself on being very organized and of being very routine oriented. He had worked hard to develop a work ethic that had served him well. In fact he had become so regimented that those who worked with him, were extremely aware of the limits he had placed on even allowing anyone to get close to him. It was very evident that they could get 'this close and no further'. Charley's quest for perfection as it would relate to guarding his 'personhood' did not result in any degree of closeness. No one really knew Charley, and Charley never got to really know anyone with whom he worked. There was great distance relationally on both sides of the equation.

Charley would arrive home from work about 5:00 p.m. just in time for supper. He was very involved in his church and taught the adult Bible class. The same emphasis on 'personal space' Charley maintained in the workplace, was evident in his home. This emphasis on personal space was developing a distance between his wife and son. This distance was heightened when attention had to be given in preparation for the Bible class. There were times when following supper; Charley would inform Sally that he had to retreat to his upstairs office to prepare his lesson. Sally and their son David were left to themselves for the large part of the evening. This was beginning to be a constant pattern, and was beginning to inflame negative relations. Week-ends became extremely busy in the attempt to give attention to everything involved in running and maintaining a home that could not be addressed during the week.

Charley and Sally entered married life as any new couple and began investigating and pursuing areas in support of each other's personhood. Sally was aware of Charley's obsessive protection of 'personal space', but early in their relationship she thought it was a passing obsession. As they continued in their relationship, it became apparent to Sally that this obsession was not lessening. In fact it was becoming more entrenched. Sally began to have serious concerns.

David's birth was a glorious occasion. This could be the breakthrough Sally was hoping would help pull Charley back from his obsession. Charley was very supportive in giving parental guidance to David. Sally was very pleased with the effort Charley gave to his role and responsibilities as David's father.

However, as David continued to grow and develop, it would appear Charley was making an assessment as to how David's needs would be better served. Charley began to pull back and Sally's load of responsibility began to increase. Sally, being the outgoing charismatic person she was, tried to downplay and even gave excuses for this apparent increase. She found herself trying to justify this outcome. It was because of the demands of Charley's job that required him to begin to 'slacken' off. At least this is the initial thought Sally began to entertain as she tried to justify Charley's actions.

It could be said that the 'writing soon appeared on the wall'. Sally had had enough. She had to speak to Charley. The decision Charley made to distance himself from the mainstream of parental responsibilities, was taking its toll on David's development not to mention Sally's struggle with the increased load. This had to be addressed.

Charley listened intently to Sally's assessment and request for him to become more involved. It was a very intense and from Sally's perspective, a very direct encounter. In some ways, Charley felt as though Sally was attacking him. The more Sally attempted to describe the struggle and concern she had, the more Charley internalized the whole ordeal.

Charley gave input from the standpoint of his heritage. It had always been this way when he was growing up. His parents, especially his father, distanced himself from the commonalities of life. He positioned himself in the role of provider as it related to providing finances. Beyond that he had the responsibility to develop and present himself as someone who had it 'all together' in the workplace.

Sally listened intently to Charley's attempt to seemingly, justify his position. This did not sit well with her. She tried her best not to condemn Charley, but how could he justify his withdrawal from family realities by placing blame on his upbringing? She asked him very point blank. "What are we going to do?" Unfortunately all Charley did was shrug his shoulders and state he didn't know. Sally being the insightful person she was, realized there was a bigger problem here than what she first thought. The encounter ended without resolution. To say there was a high degree of tension in the home would be an understatement.

Charley finally accepted the fact there was a problem,

and promised to do all he could to help resolve it. What that meant, Sally wasn't sure, but maybe it was a start. The day ended with a degree of civility.

Sally began to dissect the information Charley had shared. Charley's parents had come to faith and were active in the ministry of music. Their involvement in the church was very important in their home. The spiritual emphasis that was so important and what they had been trying to pursue did not translate or apply to building positive relations however. The family was very isolated even from their relatives. Charley had had no contact with any family member that included aunts and uncles. This had apparently gone on for a number of years, and it got to the point where it was an accepted reality. The more Sally thought of this, the more she began to understand to some extent why Charley acted the way he did.

Even though there was this isolation from their relatives, it was extremely important especially for Charley's father, to present himself as being in charge of his emotions and of his environment. He had to present himself as this person who was elevated. Is this the outcome or result of a person who has had involvement in the church for a number of years? Is this what she has to look forward to for her own family? This thought left Sally with a very bad feeling. She thought that maybe it would be a good idea to meet with her pastor and ask for his input and guidance. A meeting was arranged.

During the meeting with her pastor, Sally was very clear and descriptive as to her concern. During this meeting, Sally's family background was discussed. There was no spiritual emphasis in her family while growing up. Her parents had taken no interest in anything 'religious'. Sally was the first member of her family to come to faith. Her mother came to faith following Sally's conversion, with her father coming to faith on his deathbed. As well as describe the 'ungodly' situation that existed in her parent's home, Sally was quick to make reference to how her parents related not only to their family, but outside the home as well. Sally's parents and in particular her father, did not display any degree of trying to please someone at the expense of the family. There was no evidence of trying to be in control and having to put on a 'good face'.

One point Sally raised was very troubling. When this was brought forward, a feeling of sadness filled the room. Even though Sally's parents had not shown any interest in the things of God, their marriage withstood trials and tribulations, and they continued living as husband and wife until the day they died. It was not the same for Charley's parents. They had been involved in singing in the church for many years. Their relationship as husband and wife however, did not survive the trials and tribulations that are part and parcel of married life. After 32 years of marriage, they ended their relationship in divorce. Charley's father married again, and his mother lived alone only to contract cancer and pass away some years later.

Pastor Bailey was very quick to reassure Sally as to the importance of applying spiritual realities. It wasn't enough to merely be exposed, but there had to be an application to what you were exposed to. The intent of the meeting was not to condemn or point fingers of guilt and condemnation at Charley. Sally had arranged to meet with her pastor to try and find some way out of the dilemma that was taking place in her home with her husband.

Pastor Bailey suggested a meeting with Charley may be helpful. He asked Sally if she would support such a meeting. Sally responded very favourably, and stated she would make mention of this to Charley.

Charley listened very intently as Sally gave a rundown

of the meeting she had with Pastor Bailey. When she mentioned he would like to meet with him, she didn't know how Charley would respond. She was pleasantly surprised and relieved, when he agreed that a meeting with the pastor may be helpful. A meeting was arranged.

Pastor Bailey brought Charley 'up-to-speed' on what was discussed during his meeting with Sally. Even though the items that had been discussed pointed squarely at the position Charley was taking in the home, he did not show any discomfort. It would appear Charley was relieved to know there was some help in addressing and hopefully, resolving this situation.

Charley expressed very openly the reason why he conducted himself as he did outside the home. It was as though he had to assume a character or display a façade when in public. He did this in order to be accepted and noticed. There was an inner sense of intimidation that he constantly worked to overcome. By hiding behind this persona, he was able to find some relief. Unfortunately, he had difficulty putting that façade aside when he came home from work. This was causing grief in the relationship with Sally. Charley was very open for which Pastor Bailey was thankful. It was a clear indication that success was possible in resolving this. A meeting with both parties was suggested to which Charley was very favourable.

Upon returning home, the conversation was extremely encouraging. It was as though a breakthrough had already taken place. David joined his mom and dad in a time of thanksgiving to God for this initial breakthrough. They looked forward to a meeting being arranged.

Marital counseling was not something either of them had ever thought they would need. Pastor Bailey was very supportive and comforting. He went out of his way to relieve the apprehension he perceived. He was very clear as to the expectation and direction he would take during each session. Both Charley and Sally felt reassured. They left the first session determined to carry out any assignment faithfully.

Well into the sessions it became clear individual responsibilities would be examined. Responsibilities within the home became the focus. It was in the home where the problem really existed. Charley did not have any problem with the job he was being paid to perform. How he related to his co-workers was not the focus during the sessions with the pastor. The concern was the relationship within the home.

It was made clear that David has two parents. He has a mom and dad, and both are responsible for him. There are relational dynamics that Sally will engage in with David that are distinct from Charley's as is the reverse. Charley and David will engage in relational activities that are distinct from those of Sally and David. The roles were being confused as Sally was trying to take up the slack by engaging in relational dynamics that were reserved for Charley. This was happening because Charley had removed himself from following through and addressing those dynamics. How this shortfall was going to be addressed was for Charley to take time to be with David. Sally would need to distance herself in certain areas as well. What a shift this would be.

Charley carried through with the directives he was given with a new found enthusiasm. Charley's display of enthusiasm was so energized that it took David off guard, not to mention how taken aback Sally was. This provided a new dynamic in the home. Sally entertained the thought hoping it would last.

As the sessions continued, progress was being made that was overwhelming. It was above and beyond anything that was expected. What a time of thanksgiving ensued.

Sally began to find she had time on her hands. There were times when David was with Charley, that she was left alone. Was something developing here that they hadn't taken into account? Sally wasn't getting nervous, but she was wondering what was happening. David was responding well to this new level of involvement with his father, and Charley himself was 'coming out of himself'. This was very positive.

The progress that was being made was so positive that Pastor Bailey suggested that the sessions could be cutback. He didn't think it was necessary to continue meeting as often. They both agreed that maybe it was time to cutback. The timetable was changed with the understanding that extra sessions could be scheduled if a problem arose. The couple left the last session very uplifted in spirit.

Sally shared with Charley the increase of time she was alone, and wondered what she should do. It wasn't that she was becoming resentful, but she was finding she had to make an adjustment. Charley asked if there was anything he could do. Nothing stood out at the time, but they each said they would see what could be done. They didn't want to work at resolving one problem to have another problem surface.

During the sessions with Pastor Bailey, the application of spiritual truths in the home was stressed very aggressively. They both agreed and determined to be consistent in addressing and applying this. That determination was being rewarded with a high level of consistency. Their daily time of family devotion and prayer became extremely important.

With the changes taking place in the relationship between Sally and Charley, another change was being noticed. Charley's co-workers began to see a difference in

Charley. He didn't seem as withdrawn. He seemed to be more open and approachable. There were questions being raised among the co-workers that left them wondering just what was going on. There began to be much speculation but no one felt comfortable discussing this with him, at least, not yet.

Sally continued to enjoy her new husband. It was as though she had returned to those days when they first met. She often thought within herself that she was in a time warp, and that maybe she would wake one morning to discover reality. Whenever she had thoughts as such, she would quickly dismiss them. There was however a nagging thought that kept coming back. She thought, this would not last, that there would be a regression. She did not want to have these thoughts, but she had suffered so much before this all came to light, she didn't want to go back to what it was like before. Sally thought she should meet with Pastor Bailey.

Pastor Bailey was very quick to emphasize the importance of taking one day at a time. He stressed the need for Sally to focus on the positive. He shared with her the Scriptures that give direction to find delight in the Lord, to fill her thoughts with that which is true, that which is noble, that which is pure, that which is lovely, that which is admirable. The pastor admonished Sally through Scripture that if anything was excellent or praiseworthy; she was to think about such things. Philippians 4:4-8 (New International Version) Thoughts Sally entertained would have a bearing on how she regarded the progress being made with Charley. If she entertained negative thoughts, she would begin to zero in on that which would confirm her negative thoughts. On the other hand, if she concentrated on the positive progress that was being made, she would become encouraged with the positive progress she witnessed. This was not a mind over matter exercise. She was reminded of the words of the Apostle when writing to the church at Philippi. Paul wrote stating that our attitude, being united with Christ is to be the same as that of Christ Jesus.

Phil. 2:1-11(N.I.V.) The attitude Christ displayed was that of throwing Himself on the mercy and grace of His heavenly Father. He had complete trust and confidence in His heavenly Father. Sally was reminded that as a child of God, she can have the same confidence and trust. She is serving the One who has her best interest at heart, and invites her to throw all her care on Him because He cares for her and loves her with an everlasting love. Pastor Bailey led Sally in prayer asking God by His Holy Spirit, to remind her of His interest, and of His power to intervene and that the God she serves, does all things well. Sally left his office with thanksgiving in her heart and renewed faith and a determination to trust God.

The progression she was hoping to see in Charley was actually having a greater effect on her personally. She found that her attitude towards life in general, was extremely more positive than it had been before. Sally began to focus on positive possibilities each day. It was as though she was *looking* for the positive each day.

~~~~~~~~~~~~~~~~

Chapter Two
RELOCATION

O N THIS particular Saturday morning, Sally woke to hear an unusual sound coming from the kitchen. What was going on? Throwing on her bathrobe, she wandered into the kitchen to find Charley standing over the stove preparing breakfast. David was setting the table while Charley was 'flipping'. (flipping pancakes that is). To say Sally was taken aback would be an understatement. Charley was never comfortable in the kitchen. The further away from the kitchen he could find himself, the better.

Sally went through her morning routine and came back into the kitchen to be served breakfast. The pancakes never tasted so good. Breakfast was almost finished when Charley told both Sally and David, that they should get dressed for a trip out of town. What? Another surprise?

They got into the car and started their trip. Neither Sally nor David had any idea where they were going. As they drove along the highway, Sally began to focus on the direction and the scenery. It soon became clear that they were traveling in the same direction Charley took to his office. Charley noticed that Sally was 'cluing in' and thought he should shed some light on what he had in mind. He asked both of them if they would like to move. David responded as any ten year old would. Sally's response was more reserved. Moving from their home they had lived in for 6 years? The thought of moving from their small community where they knew just about everyone, to a larger community caused a little trepidation. Having lived in a larger community for four years prior to moving to this smaller community, Sally grew to appreciate the smallness. What was in Charley's mind?

Charley began to bring them up-to-date on what was going through his mind. He began to question if it was necessary for him to continue driving 30 minutes to work. He enjoyed driving, but the wear and tear on the car was starting to take its toil, and he thought it might be a good time to begin thinking of moving closer to work. Sally thought that yes, this does make sense.

There was yet another reason for this suggestion. As mentioned before, Charley had developed such a high quality work ethic that couldn't help but be noticed. The community service agency where he worked was preparing to expand. Their goal was to provide service and support to high need individuals that were underserved in the community. Charley was approached as to whether he would be interested in giving leadership to such an undertaking. He was given a period of time to discuss this with his family in order to get back to them with an answer.

Charley thought it would be in their best interest to live closer if he was to accept this offer.

The community, into which they would be moving, was double the size of their present location. The church of their particular denomination would be much larger. Questions of how they would fit into a larger church setting and other questions began to filter through Sally's mind. David expressed excitement with the possibility of meeting new friends. Given that David was home-schooled, the aspect of changing schools would not factor too prominently into the decision. Relocating would however, be a major decision in which they had to really be sure in getting 'the mind of the Lord'.

They drove around town for a period of time, and looked at various homes that had a for sale sign on the lawn. Charley had not made an appointment with any real estate agent at this point. He did ask Sally as they continued driving, if there was any home that really stood out as they drove by. Sally wasn't really that enthused, but she did take notice of some homes that caught her attention.

It was near time for lunch, so Charley pulled into a parking lot of a restaurant. It was a really nice restaurant. In fact it was *really* nice.

The service was second to none, and the food…..WOW!! This certainly got Sally's attention.

The drive home was very quiet. There wasn't too much conversation, but it was certainly noticed that there were many thoughts going through their minds. What were they going to do? As they were going inside their home upon their return, Charley asked both of them to really give the idea of moving serious thought. There was no further discussion until the next day.

In the meantime, Charley began to experience a feeling of insecurity and apprehension he had not experienced before. It seemed as though he was being deloused with negative thoughts that attacked his personal worth. He began to question whether he had really risen above the problem of self-importance that had caused problems between him and Sally. He questioned how David would be affected with a possible move. This and a multitude of other questions flooded Charley's mind. He was not in good shape mentally. He had to come to grips as to what he was to do in light of this new experience. Should he meet with Pastor Bailey, or work it through himself through prayer? He chose to engage in 'altar grabbing prayer'. (ref. I Kings 1:50)

He entered into a time of intercession that caused him to prostrate himself before God's throne. He experienced as never before, the fact and promise that God would answer those who call upon Him. As Charley 'stormed God's throne', God confirmed to him that He heard his plea. It was as though a weight had been lifted from his shoulders, and he began to worship the One who loved him with an everlasting love, and had his best interest at heart. Charley rose from this encounter with the reality of knowing the will of God concerning the move.

As well as coming to grips with the move to another location, Charley experienced victory over the negative feelings he had. This was a significant breakthrough.

When speaking with Sally, it became clear he was not alone in his quest for the mind of the Lord. Sally had entered into a very intense time of prayer herself, and she as well had reached the throne of God. She did not relate to the same struggle Charley had, but as she reached out to God, she received confirmation that the move was in the will of God.

David had come to faith, and knew the importance of prayer. He had also reached out to God, and had asked that his mom and dad would know what they should do.

You can imagine how charged the atmosphere was with praises of thanksgiving to God for His intervention.

Now that the decision had been made, was when challenges began.

The first thing Charley had to do was schedule a meeting with his superiors to inform them of his decision to accept their offer, and discuss other details pertinent to his decision.

Pastor Bailey was aware 'something' was in the air, and was not surprised when he was told of Charley's decision to move. When he was able to rise above the regret of Charley's decision, Pastor Bailey stated his appreciation for their support, and wanted Charley to be aware of his continued support as they prepared for this move. Even though change always creates disruption, there was no sense of being let down as Pastor Bailey reassured Charley of his continued prayer support. The search for a new Bible teacher began.

Charley secured an appointment to inform his superiors of his decision to accept their offer. Appreciation was voiced as he told them of his decision. He stated he would like to get settled in the new community before he started his new position. He was asked how long he would need. It was difficult for him to be specific as to how much time it would take for the three of them to adjust to new surroundings. He asked how much time they would be willing to give him. Due to his excellent work record, there was no need for a major discussion to answer his request. Without any hesitation, he was told he could take as much time as he needed.

As soon as Charley returned home, he told Sally the outcome of the meeting. Sally was so very thankful to know there was no time pressure, and that they would be able to 'ease' into their new surroundings. It was understood they would work to complete this resettlement as soon as possible. Sally shared with David their plans.

A myriad of tasks and details became the order of each day. Charley applied the same attention to detail that was his practice at work. It was a sight to behold to see how everything was coming together.

The area that caused the greatest challenge was regarding real estate. A real estate agent accepted eagerly the assignment to find a suitable home in the new community.

A decision had to be made as to what would become of their present home. The thought was discussed as to the value of renting out their home. The priority however, was to find a home in the new community. The financial arrangements that had to be entered into for the new home, would determine the outcome of their present home.

Was it necessary to transport everything to their new home? Is it possible that much of the 'stuff' they no longer needed could be sold? A date for a garage sale was set, and preparations for the sale were put in motion.

David was overcome with excitement. He accepted the responsibility for the placing of tables to hold the merchandise. Sally was busy pricing the items, while Charley busied himself selecting items that could be sold. This worked well until Sally saw some of the items Charley was going to sell. It was agreed that he would price the items that she chose for the sale.

You could not have asked for a better day for the sale. The weather was ideal. They had decided to hold the sale on the one Saturday, and anything that did not sell would be given to the care centre.

At the end of the day, Charley was able to put everything that did not sell, in the trunk of the car to take to the care centre. The workers were very appreciative for what they were given. The garage sale was a success.

During the Sunday morning service, Pastor Bailey called for the three of them to join him on the platform. As they stood on the platform, they heard words of appreciation and thanksgiving to God expressed by the pastor for the contribution they had made to the ministry. This was so very overwhelming for Sally. She could not contain her emotions any longer and began to cry. She had given herself wholeheartedly to the ladies group and friendships were developed that went beyond the meeting time. She was going to miss that.

David as well became emotional. He had surrounded himself with those his age that became close to him.

A bouquet of flowers was given to Sally just before Charley was asked to share, and a gift was given to David. Pastor Bailey leaned over the railing behind the platform, and presented Charley with a plaque with the inscription that expressed appreciation for the contribution and blessing he had been to that congregation. Charley struggled to regain his composure as he began to share.

Just before he began to speak, Sally nodded that she would like to say something. She took the microphone and began to express her appreciation for the grace and mercy of God, and for the support she had received since coming to this church. She went on to say how she will miss the contact with those she has come to love and appreciate. She emphasized the fact they would not be moving so far away that she wouldn't be able to visit from time to time. She finished her comments by asking for prayer as they settle into their new community.

Charley expressed thanks for the support he had personally received from Pastor Bailey. With the revelation of the inner struggle that had been going on for an undetermined period of time, Pastor Bailey had been used of God to give guidance and an experience of victory ensued for which he will be eternally grateful. He went on to say that through the grace, mercy and intervention by the Spirit of God, he has been able to look beyond his own needs and interests. Because of this breakthrough within his own heart, he is looking forward to 'coming-along-side' others to be a channel of blessing to assist others in moving beyond their needs, in order to be of help and support. This has been a breakthrough that continues to have a positive effect in every area of his life. This includes not only his relationship at work, but his relationship with his wife and son. There cannot be enough said of what an impact this has had and continues to have in many areas of his life. He asked for prayer as they not only relocate, but as he starts this new area of ministry.

Pastor Bailey asked the congregation to stand, and asked the three of them to stand before the altar and for board members to stand beside them as he prepared to lead in prayer. As prayer was offered on behalf of this family, the reality of the presence of God filled that sanctuary beyond description.

What a tremendous display of support from this family of faith.

Unbeknown to the three of them, a gathering was planned following the morning service. A farewell dinner had been prepared giving members of the congregation, more personal opportunity to say 'good-bye' to this family. My- Oh- My, more surprises for this family.

More presentations and expressions of appreciation were given to the extent that the three of them felt so overwhelmed. Words to express their heartfelt appreciation were hard to find. What a send-off!

Monday was very busy as effort began to be put forth in preparing for the move.

It was proving to be very interesting as they tried to put up with the absolute minimal of clothing and supplies. They had packed everything they could. They now waited with baited breath for a call from the real estate agent.

They were very thankful they didn't have to wait too long to receive that call. A meeting with the agent was arranged, and they were shown a number of homes the agent thought would be suitable.

The three homes they had been shown were nice, but something was missing. What would this fourth home look like? Would this be the home, or would they have to go through this exercise again? They followed the agent to the front of this nice looking home in what appeared to be a nice section of the town. They went inside and it seemed to resonate within the three of them, that this was the house. Details were discussed with the real estate agent, and another showing was arranged.

The drive home was filled with extreme excitement. It is hard to express the level of excitement that seemed to 'pour' out of the three of them. You can imagine the excitement David expressed. The home they would be moving into was a three bedroom bungalow with a completed basement. The home had been taken care of and was in immaculate shape. Charley envisioned keeping in shape physically, as he assessed what would be required in maintaining the lawn. David in all likelihood would be assigned some involvement in this area. Sally's thoughts centered around the interior of the home as she envisioned changes she would probably make. Some of the rooms became a blur in her mind. She would need to go into the home again in order to separate and identify in more detail what changes she would like to make.

Needless to say, the next period of time was filled with a high degree of excitement and preparation.

Another opportunity to visit their 'new' home was arranged with more intense attention being given to each room, and the home in general.

Discussion centered on the fate of their present home. It became very clear that they would not be able to maintain their present home. A meeting was arranged to determine the worth of their home, with a selling price being determined. Their home was placed on the market.

Even though there had been no time pressure placed on them for their move and settlement into the community, they did not want this to drag out longer than it should.

They wanted the house to sell as quickly as possible so

they would be able to move into their new home. The acceptance offer for their new home was contingent on the sale of their present home. The 'dovetailing' of the two real estate situations was sought and looked forward to. There was no doubt in their minds that God was already at work in bringing this all together. It is certainly refreshing and encouraging seeing a family within the community of faith, taking such a positive position of faith and confidence in the God they serve. What a testimony to the grace and mercy of God.

This positive position continued to overshadow the three of them as they maintained their consistent daily dependency on the strength and provision of God through prayer and supplication. They each experienced the reality that the God they served was able and willing to do above and beyond anything they had thought of or imagined. Reality? Yes! Were there periods of uncertainty? Of apprehension? Yes! But when they called on God in prayer, the Spirit of God moved in and filled those moments of doubt and apprehension with an awareness that He is faithful and can be counted on to do all things well for His honour and glory. They continued to accept the fact that all things work together for good, to them who loved God, to them who are called according to His purpose.

Rom. 8:28.

There was it seemed, a steady stream of traffic coming and going through their home as many came to inspect the house. This constant barrage of people visiting their home did make for disruption, but there was no complaining.

Listen to hear the outcome of a telephone conversation Sally had with the real estate agent. Charley and David were outside when the phone rang. "Hello, yes this is

Sally. I'm sorry, would you repeat that please? You have an offer for the home, and it was the exact price we were asking? Oh my, let me get my husband".

Charley came to the phone, and he was a little more reserved than Sally, but at the same time very excited. There was an offer for their home. Arrangements were made for the agent to bring the offer for signing. The fact that their home sold, allowed them to contact the real estate agent to complete the paperwork required for their new home. Arrangements were made with a moving company in preparation for the move.

Was it really necessary for such a large moving van to be used for the move? It was surprising when the last piece of furniture and other items were placed in the van, that it was full.

It was time to get in the car and begin the drive to their new home.

Excitement was so keen that it seemed to take forever to arrive at their new home. They arrived before the moving van, and were able to relax a little before the moving van arrived. Sally made arrangements with a local caterer for lunch to be delivered. The movers were very appreciative for this gesture.

It didn't take as long to unload the van as Charley thought it would take. The van was emptied, and the furniture was put in place quite quickly, and they were so thankful that nothing was broken. What a tremendous move. Now the work really began.

They thought to 'ease' into the new community by just taking their time in adjusting. This meant they would forestall and put off any commitment of time for any undertaking until they felt it was the 'right' time for them. They wanted to be sure of where they would be 'lead' to serve. Prayer and supplication continued to be a daily practice as they settled into their new environment.

The first week seemed to fly by. Here it was one week since they had made the initial move, and they had settled into their new home quite well. In fact, the house looked as though they had been there longer than just a week. Sally had really worked hard in putting her stamp on the interior. David had taken ownership of his room and it certainly looked like his room. The attention Charley gave to the exterior gave right upfront commitment, that they would be an asset to the community. The interior of the garage didn't look too shabby either.

The first service they attended in what would be their new church, was quite different from what they had grown accustomed to in their previous location. Everything was so energized. They each found themselves looking around, trying to take in as much as they could. What a difference.

At the conclusion of the service as they were preparing to leave, they were approached by different members of the congregation that went out of their way to welcome them. The pastor made his presence felt, and enthusiastically shook their hands and stated how pleased he was to have them visiting. He was not aware of the particulars that brought them to that service.

When they arrived home from the service, they prepared for their meal. They each shared their initial impression of their first service in what would be their new church. One area they each found overwhelming was the large congregation. What a difference a large congregation made in every aspect of the service. Sally made reference to the large number of ladies her age in attendance. David as well took notice of how many 'kids' were there. Charley hesitated before giving his input. He expressed surprise that Pastor Bailey had not informed their new pastor of their arrival. He thought that the new pastor would have been told of this new family that would be moving into the area, and of how involved they had been in his church.

Interestingly enough, when Sally heard his remarks, she made a mental note. She thought within herself that she would have to bring this to his attention after David had left the table and they were alone.

The meal was over, the table cleared, the dishes were put in the dishwasher and David went off to his room. Now was a good time to speak with Charley.

"What were you thinking when you expressed disappointment with Pastor Bailey? We are not important representatives that have been given some diplomatic assignment Charley. We have to be careful we don't go back to the problem of self-importance we struggled with before". What a revealing rebuke! Because Sally offered her concern from a heart of sincerity before God, there was no caustic fallout that caused him to be defensive. He took the voiced concern in the spirit it was given. He expressed sorrow and agreed with Sally that he would have to be aware of how he came across. He stated further that the concern was his alone and not her concern or David's. He was the one who had displayed that 'sort of image' before, and He would have to seek the help of God in not reverting back. He thanked Sally for her insight and expressed thanksgiving to God for blessing him with such an insightful and loving wife.

Sally was busy in the kitchen and was waiting for David to join her, when the phone rang. It was Pastor Cornwall. During the conversation, he told her that he tries to make the initial contact with those who filled out the contact card from Sunday services. He asked if he could forward their name to the chairperson of the fellowship committee, who would contact them to arrange a visit. This was met with enthusiasm. Charley welcomed this news with enthusiasm as well. They didn't have to wait long for a meeting to be arranged. A meeting was arranged for Thursday evening. David was invited to attend the meeting as well.

Mr. and Mrs. Shepherd had been serving at Glad Tidings for a number of years, and have been so very thankful for the opportunity of being an extension of the ministry. They provide the initial contact with new people coming into the church. Those who have indicated interest in becoming knowledgeable in the span of ministry at Glad Tidings, meet with the fellowship representatives as this family was doing.

This meeting gave them the opportunity to share the degree of involvement they had under Pastor's Bailey's ministry. They were asked if they had any concern with Pastor Bailey being contacted on their behalf. There was no concern voiced. In fact, this provided a point of safety for Charley. He was spared the temptation to 'blow his own horn'. This caused a note of thanksgiving to be presented to God from both of them.

The information they received was very helpful. There were several areas of ministry at Glad Tidings that both Charley and Sally could become interested in. There was as well a good and thriving youth program that would be of interest to David.

After the Shepherds left, they each spent time discussing possibilities of involvement in the church. David was very keen on pursuing the youth ministry program as it was presented by the Shepherds. There was so much to consider as they continued to settle in.

~~~~~~~~~~~~~~~~~

Chapter Three
NEW HORIZONS

C HARLEY BEGAN to formulate the approach in developing the service to high need individuals. It is very challenging to start a new approach from ground zero. There were times when Charley felt the weight of the challenge, but was very enthused with the opportunity.

While there hadn't been a strong spiritual emphasis at his last 'post', he thought to place emphasis on the spiritual component to this new adventure. He sought to discuss this with his superiors. During the meeting, he began to outline the new thrust and direction in which he would like to take this new venture. His input received rapt attention. While there was an understanding and general acceptance of Charley's 'spiritual' position during the time he worked in the office, there had never been any overt display or discussion of spirituality.

Once again, due to Charley's work ethic and the high regard in which he was held in the eyes of those he worked with, there did not appear to be any hesitation in supporting this approach. This was at least the initial position being taken.

He concluded his presentation and stated he would welcome any and all feedback. The meeting concluded with thanks being expressed to Charley for his leadership.

He left the meeting sensing within himself that he will receive comments when this new approach has 'sunk in'.

During the next period of time, Charley continued assessing and developing a strategy in reaching those of the community needing assistance. This was taking on a bigger challenge than what he first thought. Perhaps a meeting with Pastor Cornwall would be of help.

Charley began to share with Pastor Cornwall just what he was purposing to develop in this new community. He asked if there was any area of particular concern. The answer he received was very surprising. It was initially thought that those of the community needing extra support would be developmentally challenged individuals as well as those commonly called, 'street people'. Pastor Cornwall stated his concern with those within his congregation who exhibited isolation and self-centeredness. What a statement! And to think it was coming from the pastor of a large church. Charley did his best not to show his surprise. Was this a confirmation that the move was absolutely the right move for them? Was this reassurance that what they (and particular Charley himself) had experienced before, was to equip them in being of support to others who were going through the same thing? To think he had been delivered from an obsession of self-importance and self-centeredness, only to be informed of others who were in need of deliverance from the same obsession. This had to be regarded as Divine preparedness.

Charley did not share with Pastor Cornwall his experience in dealing with this concern. He thought he would just listen to what the pastor was describing, and would just leave it with the Lord to indicate when he should share his experience.

Charley informed Pastor Cornwall that he would keep him informed as to developments, and asked for prayer support as he embarked on this endeavour.

Charley continued giving thought to how he should go about developing this new ministry. He was reminded of an organization in a large metropolitan area that was giving support to developmentally challenged individuals. He thought to contact them for guidance and information. A meeting was arranged.

He had to drive about an hour from his home to meet with leaders of this organization. The name of the organization pointed very clearly to their course of action and emphasis. The name of this organization was Eternal Perspective. This left no doubt as to what they were all about. The ministry of Eternal Perspective was conducted within a trans-denominational setting. They operated independently from any church-based organization, and received financial support through gifts and government assistance from those in their care.

Charley found this introduction to be very informative and helpful. He left the meeting with the thought that he should visit one of the homes. Another meeting was scheduled.

When he arrived home, he seemed pre-occupied with the information he had been given. When speaking with Sally, he wondered how he could go about incorporating the approach this 'ministry' took, into his development. He did appear much focused when sharing this with Sally.

Adjustment to the community and what it offered continued to be the focus for the three of them. It was interesting to see how they each went about investigating what appealed to their individual needs and interests. This was certainly an exciting time for them as they continued to adjust.

Charley was able to visit one of the homes of Eternal Perspective, and following the visit, he met with the leaders of this ministry. He shared with them his plans and objectives in developing a support program in his community. You can imagine his surprise when he was told that they had been giving thought to expanding into his community. They had only reached the discussion stage and no effort had been put forth to go any further. That is, until meeting Charley.

It was stated that development of their approach to offering support to high need individuals beyond areas in which they were presently established, would provide smoother development if it was an extension or what was already established. What he was hearing in essence, was the question; "Why reinvent the wheel?"

Charley was asked if he would be interested in becoming part of their organization and ministry. After getting over the initial shock of the question, he responded that he would certainly give it serious thought. He would however, appreciate a fuller understanding of the mandate and focus of this ministry.

Eternal Perspective can be taken as a highly ambitious term. Charley asked for clarification.

He was told that the focus of the ministry was birthed from the need to 'come-along-side' those in the community who struggled with issues of life. It became quite clear as intense investigation ensued, that those who struggled were disenfranchised by the mainstream of the society in which they lived. There was separation and a sense of second class citizenship in the minds of those who struggled.

The founders of Eternal Perspective became burdened as they saw the need for the hand of God to be extended to those in need. They recognized and accepted the reality that God has no hands but their hands, and that He was preparing to reach out to those in need.

Eternal Perspective positions itself with a boundless unceasing mindset and outlook on the eternal worth of individuals for whom Christ died.

The meeting concluded with Charley's verbal commitment to investigate the possibility of joining their ranks.

The drive home was a very thought provoking experience. He could hardly wait to tell Sally.

Sally listened very intently to what Charley was sharing with her. Man Oh Man, more things to think about, with more decisions to be made. Talk about an exciting life-style. This would certainly fall under that category.

They both agreed to take the matter before the Lord in prayer, and once again, seek His face.

Charley received a phone call from one of his supervisors inviting him to attend a meeting. This was interesting. Charley wondered what this was all about.

As he entered the room, the same individuals that were at the last meeting, were present. They welcomed Charley and were pleasant, but there was an air of something that just didn't sit well with him.

It became clear there had been serious thought and discussion on Charley's proposal in the development of a 'ministry' aspect to his assignment. There was no down and out rejection or ridicule of Charley's spiritual goals and life-style, but comments of unsettledness were brought forward. It was suggested that instead of developing and establishing homes for the developmentally challenged individuals under the 'Christian' banner, that the establishment of a food bank would provide a more neutral position.

This food bank could be established to provide food to 'street people' without any spiritual connotation.

Charley listened very intently to the comments that were shared. When asked for his input, he stated that the establishment of a food bank was certainly less than he was prepared to develop. He felt that those in the community requiring more intensive support would be overlooked. He did not feel this would be in his best interest nor would it give the support needed for the most vulnerable and needy in the community. He was not relegating the 'street people' to the classification of not having intense needs, but there were other organizations already engaged in addressing this need.

He did conclude his remarks by stating he would like to have time to give this more thought. He asked if he could get back to them with a decision. This request was granted as he left the meeting.

The question of "What am I to do?" continued to resonate through his being.

Throughout the remaining day and into the evening, he continued to be deluged with thoughts that centered on both scenarios. What would it be like to develop a food bank? What would it be like to work for Eternal Perspective? What would the Lord have me to do?

Charley entered into a very intense time of prayer and supplication seeking direction. He was not given to seeking 'signs', but he did ask that God would give him definite confirmation as to His will in this matter.

When discussing this with Sally, her response was that he had to do what was in his heart, and what he felt was the Lord's leading. As well, he should give serious thought to what would be in the best interest of those he was sent to serve.

During this time of deliberation, he felt a compulsion to meet with Pastor Cornwall. A meeting was arranged.

It was during this meeting that Charley shared with his new pastor, the experience he had some time ago, before moving into the new community. Pastor Cornwall listened intently. When he had brought Pastor Cornwall up to date on his present challenge, he wondered if there would be any way for some involvement from the church. Eternal Perspective positions itself as a ministry within a trans-denominational setting, and is in truth, an extension of the community of faith.

Pastor Cornwall was aware of this group and focus of their ministry, and assured Charley that he would bring this forward during the board meeting. He did ask Charley for more information as to how much support he would need from the church. Charley said he would get back to him as he was able, to identify the level of support he would need.

Charley was clearly and definitely at a crossroads, but it was becoming clear where the Lord was leading him. He began to experience a deep settled peace within his spirit. The direction of the Holy Spirit was becoming clear to Charley.

It is amazing what takes place when we are faced with a major decision, and are open to the guidance and direction of the Holy Spirit. Charley took note of the concern Pastor Cornwall shared in reference to some members of his congregation, during the first meeting he had with his new pastor. There were those who appeared to be very self-centered. This was the struggle Charley had before being visited by the Spirit of God. This comment came back to Charley as he deliberated and pondered his decision. Reference to this comment raised another level of investigation for Charley.

He continued giving serious thought and deliberation to the whole range of possibilities that faced him. Interestingly enough, there was no sense of anxiety within Charley. In fact he was very calm both inwardly as well as externally. He told Sally one evening as they were about to have their family prayer time, that he was going to work with Eternal Perspective. What took Sally completely off guard, was what Charley continued to share with her. Not only was Charley going to work with this new ministry, but he was also going to investigate the possibility of working with Pastor Cornwall.

Once again, there was no element of trepidation. There was no feeling of launching out on quick sand. It was a matter of Sally asking Charley, "When are you going to start?" She did not have any questions of doubt. Amazing!

The following morning before he left for work, he called his office and spoke with his superiors. He asked to have a meeting with them. He was told that they would be able to meet with him later that morning. This was exactly what Charley was hoping for.

Charley had no sooner finished his conversation with his work that the phone rang. It was Pastor Cornwall. He had spoken with the Board members, and they were very enthused with the possibility of Charley becoming involved in ministry at Glad Tidings. He asked Charley when they could meet. Charley suggested meeting in the afternoon. This was agreed to.

Charley did not hesitate in the least as he entered the meeting room. He was very pleasant, and did not waste any time stating his decision. He stated very clearly his appreciation for the time he had worked with them, and of how thankful he was for their guidance and support. There was a longing within him that was driving him to branch out and become more directly involved in Christian ministry. He stated he would relinquish his position with the firm immediately. Due to the fact that there was very limited development of the new approach, there was no need to train anyone. This being the case, there was no need to give an extensive notice of termination.

When Charley had finished giving his announcement, the one in charge gave his input. He began stating his appreciation for Charley as a person, and of his tremendous work ethic. He had certainly been an asset to the work. Even though they are sorry to learn of Charley's decision, it was not a surprise.

They wished Charley well, and stated he did not have to distance himself from making contact with them whenever. They shook Charley's hand, and again wished him well.

Charley left the meeting, unemployed.

Upon entering the board room at Glad Tidings, Charley was welcomed with enthusiasm he had not experienced for a long time. Each board member welcomed him and embraced him as a member of the family.

Pastor Cornwall welcomed Charley to the meeting, and asked him to share what the Lord had laid on his heart.

Charley began by expressing his pleasure and gratitude in being able to meet with them. He also shared his appreciation and that of his wife and son of being so warmly received at Glad Tidings. Charley continued to share his experience that had a direct impact on his decision to become more involved at Glad Tidings. Charley did not share the comment Pastor Cornwall had made regarding those in the congregation that he felt were struggling with self-centeredness. He approached his decision to become more involved from the standpoint of being lead. It was as though God was plotting a course of action and involvement for him. There was no doubt that what was birthed in his heart was in the providence of God.

Pastor Cornwall interjected with his response to the initial conversation he and Charley had regarding the possibility of Charley receiving support from the church. The issue of support was left open as to what this support would consist of. Pastor Cornwall thought to bring this forward so there would be no misunderstanding of the intent of the meeting and of Charley's involvement.

The chairman of the board proceeded to give his input. He had met with Pastor Cornwall and they had discussed the need for someone of Charley's ability and dedication to give leadership. There had been contact with Pastor Bentley who had given them valuable insight concerning Charley. Especially as it related to the support and commitment they would receive from him.

Charley thanked the members of the board for their endorsement, and emphasized his purpose as only to be a vessel used for the glory of God.

The meeting closed with prayer with the board members gathering around Charley asking for God's richest blessing and guidance to be given to him. Pastor Cornwall would be introducing Charley to the congregation the following Sunday, as the newest member of the ministry team.

The drive home was filled with thanksgiving for the intervention of the Spirit of God in bringing this all together. He could hardly wait to tell Sally and David.

Upon returning home, Charley told Sally he had great news to share, but before he could take time to bring her up-to-date, he had to make a call to Eternal Perspective.

"Hello, yes, could I speak with Mr. Patterson please? Hello, Mr. Patterson, this is Charley Butterworth. Oh, I'm fine thank you. I'm calling to let you know that I would look forward to working with Eternal Perspective, and hope the opportunity is still being offered to me. Yes, I could start tomorrow. That is great Mr. Patterson. I'll look forward to seeing you in the morning. Thank you".

Charley got off the phone and hugged both Sally and David. A new day was to begin for the three of them, and especially for Charley.

He began to share what had taken place during the meeting with Pastor Cornwall and the board members. Both Sally and David listened with rapt attention. When Charley has finished giving them this update, they were speechless. My-Oh-My!! What God is doing!

~~~~~~~~~~~~~~~~~~~~

Chapter Four
LAUNCHING OUT

C HARLEY WOKE quite early, and prepared to meet with his new boss to begin his new job. The drive was not in the least bit arduous. In fact, he found it quite enjoyable. He was looking forward to this new beginning.

Mr. Patterson gave Charley a warm welcome, and worked to lessen any apprehension he may have by letting him know, he would prefer if Charley would address him by his first name; Bruce.

Details addressing expectations, salary, time commitments, etc. were laid out before Charley. It was evident that preparation had been made for his arrival and acceptance for the position. There was really no need for further explanation. Everything was extremely clear. He is to meet with Bruce each Friday morning initially for the next period of time, for support and any guidance that may be necessary. This time commitment would be cut-back as he becomes more entrenched. He spent the remainder of the day meeting other staff members, and becoming familiar with the rationale and approach that is being taken in giving care and support to those in need.

Driving home, Charley toyed with the idea of where he would set up an office. Initially, he would be content to work out of his home, but this would definitely be a short-term arrangement. He would begin to search for an appropriate location as soon as possible.

Sally worked closely with David in continuing the approach that was in place for his in-home education. In the back of Sally's mind was some trepidation. Charley had responded well to the guidance and direction he had been given by Pastor Bentley. He had accepted the need to share parental responsibilities with Sally, but with the extended work load confronting Charley, she wondered if this would give cause for Charley to distance himself again.

When Charley arrived home, he asked if Sally would like to join him for a cup of coffee. She accepted the invitation and called for David to join them.

Charley filled them in with the details of his meeting with Bruce, and approached the challenge of setting up an office in the basement. He asked David to give him a hand in this endeavour. David just beamed with excitement of being asked to be part of this project. Sally was offering thanksgiving inwardly for this display of Charley's continued acceptance of his parental responsibility to David.

Charley also shared with them his need to develop a schedule that would assist him in giving appropriate time for everything that was 'on his plate'. He stated that he will draw up a schedule and get their input on it.

Saturday began with an exceptional degree of activity. They had breakfast and entered into a time of reflection on the goodness and faithfulness of God. They each shared from their heart thanksgiving to God for all He had done since they had made their move to this new community. Their time of family devotion was filled with expressions of praise.

Sally had made an appointment at the hair dressers

and asked if there was anything she needed to get on her way back. Neither of them thought of anything. Charley and David began to address the challenge of setting up the office.

When Sally returned, she was overcome with surprise as she saw the result of the time Charley and David had spent in getting the office in shape. In fact, she could hardly believe her eyes! "How did you guys get so far in such a short time? I wasn't gone that long." Charley smiled and said that he had a good helper.

Sally began to prepare the supper meal while David busied himself in his room, and Charley began to cut the grass. What a busy household!

When the meal was finished and the kitchen was tidied, they each headed for the living-room to relax. What a day it had been!

Nothing else took place needing physical output. They were anxious to get to bed.

Following the offering and announcements, Pastor Bailey began to share the latest development with the congregation. He announced that the board had invited Charley to become a member of the ministry team at Glad Tidings. He invited Charley to join him on the platform. Charley then expressed his appreciation and requested prayer that his input and contribution would serve to bring honour to the Lord, and encouragement and support to the ministry at Glad Tidings. Pastor Cornwall then led in prayer and began to share from the Word of God.

The rest of the day was spent relaxing and enjoying the beautiful weather. They went for a walk to take in the scenery in their neighbourhood, and they met some of their neighbours. It was a good day.

Monday began quite early for Charley. He had determined that he would begin his day very early to use that time for spiritual maintenance, development and preparation. The more he was able to accomplish before setting out, would guard against taking time away from Sally and David. As well, by starting his day as early as he planned, would allow him to focus on the task at hand without interruption with phone calls.

He sought as well to establish a pattern that would serve to help Sally and David develop a schedule. The management of time is of major importance to avoid wasting time.

He purposed to develop a written work schedule so that Sally and David would know when he was 'at work' and could not be disturbed. Charley realized that preparing a written schedule could appear to be very 'cold and cut-and-dry', but there was too much at stake to address time issues less responsibly.

Sally and David started their day with a determined focus as well. Sally had helped establish in David's young mind, the need for time management. With being home-schooled, there was the temptation to 'go-with-the-flow' and not zero-in on any particular goal and objectives. David had set personal goals to which he was targeting, and avoided the temptation to 'go with the flow'.

As well as to ensure David was addressing his personal goals and interests, Sally began to address her personal priorities as well. When living in their previous community, she had become quite involved with other parents who were involved with home-schooling. She wondered how she would go about meeting such a group in her new community.

As young as David was, he was becoming very adept with computers. He had completed various courses and had shown tremendous skill and interest in programming. This was certainly of encouragement to both Sally and Charley.

David spent large 'chunks of time' developing greater skill levels. Both parents were so thankful that his skill level and interest, took him beyond video games.

Charley addressed the development of the ministry of Eternal Perspective as aggressively as he could, and set out to review the market for such an approach.

He introduced himself to the Community of Social Services. This service organization was aware of Eternal Perspective, and their particular focus. While the 'Christian' emphasis was viewed with some skepticism, the value and worth of the organization was held in high regard. Charley realized early on that his responsibility was to maintain the high standard of excellence that had been established.

Charley set out to secure an office where he could in-terview possible staff for this venture. He thought that maybe Pastor Cornwall would allow him the use of an office at the church to hold these interviews.

Pastor Cornwall did not hesitate at all when Charley made the request. In fact, he was told that the office he was going to use for interviews, would serve as his per-sonal office as a member of the ministry team. Charley was so very thankful. After obtaining a post office box, he put together an appeal for staff who would work in a residential setting, giving care and support for develop-mentally challenged adults. An ad was placed in the local paper.

The process was now 'in motion' towards developing an extension of the ministry of External Perspective in a new community.

Charley began to investigate real estate possibilities. This effort was very involved due to the required partic-ulars needed for such a home. An appointment was made with a real estate agent. During the initial appointment,

Charley outlined expectations and demands for the type of home that was required. The agent accepted his assignment without hesitation.

Now that two major steps were in place, Charley gave attention to preparing his weekly schedule for Sally and David.

As well as giving attention to this task, he began giving thought to the direction and focus of his ministry at Glad Tidings.

Pastor Cornwall made his way to Charley's office, knocked at the door, and was invited in. This encounter proved to be very timely.

Pastor Cornwall began to outline for Charley specifics that helped address the focus of his role of a member of the ministry team.

He proceeded to invite Charley to the weekly pastoral meeting held each Tuesday morning. It is at this meeting that all aspects of the ministry of Glad Tidings are discussed. As well, Charley listened very intently as Pastor Cornwall outlined the specific area of ministry he would like Charley to address.

Charley would be responsible to conduct weekly Bible studies. This assignment would be more involved than the traditional Bible study that would normally be conducted during the Christian Education hour Sunday morning. Pastor Cornwall reiterated the substance of the conversation he had had with Charley some time ago. It was during this conversation, that he had shared his concern with the struggle members of the congregation were experiencing. This struggle was very apparent to Pastor Cornwall, and he felt Charley had come to Glad Tidings according to Divine Providence to help address this concern.

He was confident that God had directed Charley to assist him in addressing this particular need. This information was not given as a means of elevating Charley, but the sincerity with which Pastor Cornwall shared 'his heart', spoke volumes to Charley.

Before leaving, Pastor Cornwall asked if he could have a word of prayer. The emphasis Pastor Cornwall placed on prayer was extremely evident and much appreciated. Charley experienced such tremendous spiritual support that left him overwhelmed.

After Pastor Cornwall left, Charley found himself so aware of the presence of God that he had to stop and just bask in this reality.

This Monday was certainly a break from a traditional Monday. There was no 'easing' into the week. This work week started with a 'bang'.

Where did the time go? Here it was nearing 4:00. He certainly did not want to be late getting home. He was looking forward to telling Sally and David of the tremendous day he had. What a day!

As Charley was coming into the house and getting ready to put his feet up before supper, both Sally and David accosted him asking how his first day on the job went. He started right away telling them that they would not believe the day he had. He proceeded to share the happenings of the day as they began to be seated at the supper table. The meal continued much longer than usual. There was so much to share. When Charley finally brought them up-to-speed, he asked how their day went.

Sally stated; "You think you had a great day? Wait until you hear how our day went". Sally had come in contact with the group that addressed home-schooling issues. Apparently, they were very supportive of each other and met at least once a month for support and encouragement.

David came in contact with a computer service that was very interested in his skill level. There was mention of the possibility of David creating programs for their clients.

Following this very involved supper, they entered into their time of family devotion. They each expressed appreciation and thanksgiving to God for His guidance and provision throughout the day.

Charley gave both Sally and David, a copy of his proposed schedule. He would work 8-4 Monday to Thursday with Eternal Perspective. On Friday, he would meet with Bruce Patterson, but this would not tie up the whole day. Friday evening, Saturday and Sunday would be set aside for Sally and David.

Thursday night was reserved for the Bible study.

Wednesday night was reserved for the weekly prayer meeting.

Sally expressed appreciation for the work Charley had put into this schedule, and she was aware there would come occasions when changes would have to be made, but she was thankful for the foundation Charley had laid.

David would be part of the youth program that runs Friday night.

Sally would pursue the ladies' program that runs Tuesday night.

They were each rather tired but enthused with what had taken place. It was an exciting day.

Tuesday started with a little apprehension taking root in Charley's mind. This would be the first time he would meet with the full ministry team. He approached his time of meditation and personal Bible reading with an intensity that elevated the reality of the presence of God within his spirit.

He left the house following breakfast with anticipation as he looked forward to this meeting. The meeting was scheduled to begin at 9:00. Before the meeting was to start, he familiarized himself with what needed to be addressed with Eternal Perspective later that day.

Charley was introduced to each member of the team. He met the Worship Leader, the Youth Leader, the Director of Christian Education, and the Chairperson of the Fellowship committee. When introductions were completed, Pastor Cornwall opened the meeting with prayer.

Charley was asked if there was any direct guidance being given to him in regards to Thursday night. Charley began to share what would be the initial focus of the Thursday night study.

The thrust of the study would centre around the need to refocus on a majestic perspective. This would assist in making the move from the mundane level of relationship with God that can result in stagnation, to the level of interaction with the Spirit of God that will lift one to higher heights and deeper depths in a relationship with our Heavenly Father. This would be a process that those attending the study, would hopefully engage in.

The response from the other members was very encouraging. This gave Charley a sense of acceptance from his peers. He left the meeting with the understanding that they were each on the 'same page' with the same determination to do all for the glory of God.

Sally and David began their day following breakfast, with a time of devotion and prayer. Following this time, David headed to his bedroom, with Sally going into the kitchen. She was anxious to have everything finished around the house so she would be able to attend the meeting that evening. This would be the first ladies meeting she would attend since joining Glad Tidings.

David spent the morning in front of the computer, but was anxious to have lunch as the energy he had put forth working on the computer needed to be replaced. Besides, he wanted to get some fresh air. Despite David's youth, he had developed a good sense of priorities. To the surprise of both his parents, David had shown a keen interest in gardening. He had sectioned off a corner of the property where he had planted seeds for growing vegetables. Neither Sally nor Charley was aware David had a 'green thumb'. This discovery was most interesting.

Charley continued his day developing the approach he would take to introduce the community to the ministry of Eternal Perspective. The appeal for residential workers would appear in the local newspaper on Wednesday.

Charley continued to work on the introduction of the Bible study. He had targeted the first session to take place the following Thursday. He worked to develop an announcement informing the congregation of the subject matter, and the thrust of the study. This was completed along with an overhead transparency.

When Charley arrived home, he found Sally busy in the kitchen getting supper ready. David was setting the table. There was an air of busyness in the home as Charley settled in. Sally stated she was looking forward to her first meeting with the ladies.

There wasn't too much conversation regarding Charley's day. His day was filled with preparation for both Eternal Perspective as well as preparing the introduction for the Majestic Perspective study.

Following supper, they entered into a time of family devotion and prayer. This time continues to be very special for each of them.

The table was cleared with the kitchen being cleaned up, as Sally put the finishing touches on her appearance as she prepared to attend the meeting. Charley asked David what he had worked on through the day. David took him into his 'computer centre' and proceeded to detail his progress. Charley was very impressed, and listened with rapt attention as David outlined developments.

David then closed down the computer and told his dad

he had something else to show him. "Come outside Dad". Charley followed David to the corner of the yard where he had planted his garden. Needless to say, Charley's mouth dropped open in amazement and surprise. "When did you plant this David?" "A few days ago", was his reply. All Charley could say was, "Wow".

He asked David if there were any other surprises. David smiled and said, "No".

Charley left David examining his garden as he went into the house and proceeded to prepare a cup of coffee. He then sat in the living-room and began reading the paper. He presented a very relaxed picture.

David came into the living-room with a glass of fruit juice. As he sat down, Charley asked him how he was enjoying his new home. David responded by stating that he was really glad they had moved, but that he was anxious to meet some new kids and make some friends. He was looking forward to attending the youth meeting on Friday night.

The evening was spent by engaging in various items of discussion, but with no serious overtones. They were both relaxed as they waited for Sally to return.

The meeting was everything Sally had hoped it would be. The ladies had gathered around her, and made her feel right at home. She was even able to make contact with a few of the mothers who were involved in home-schooling. This was extremely helpful.

Sally began to share various aspects of the meeting, and both Charley and David could see how much Sally enjoyed the meeting.

The evening ended on a very positive note, but they were glad to be able to retire. It seemed to be a long day.

Wednesday began without incident as Charley addressed what had become, his morning routine. He had breakfast, and left for his office. He stopped and purchased a copy of the local newspaper, and looked for his ad. Everything was worded as he had given it, and the ad was actually placed in a strategic location on the page. He was hoping it would stimulate a good response.

It was not long after he had reached his office that the phone rang. He was pleased to find that it was the real estate agent calling to tell him he had found a number of possible locations for the home he was seeking. A time was arranged for Charley to inspect these homes.

The homes appeared to be suitable with minor adjustments having to be made. Charley stated he would need to discuss this with his superiors, and would be meeting with them on Friday. The agent was very accommodating.

Charley returned to his office and resumed preparation for both aspects of his ministry.

The day ended with a number of accomplishments being made that allowed him to consider the day to be a success.

He made his way home anticipating a delicious supper. For some reason, he was quite hungry.

As he expected, Sally had been very busy preparing for this important meal, and the aroma of the prepared meal, caused Charley's taste buds to stand at attention.

After finishing this delicious meal, Sally reminded Charley of the prayer meeting scheduled for that evening. This caused a moment of hesitation in Charley's mind. It would be great if the three of them could attend, but there was the question of whether David should attend. He was asked if he would like to attend the prayer meeting. Without hesitation, his response was "Yes".

The three of them left to attend the prayer meeting.

David continues to display a real hunger and desire for the things of God.

Pastor Cornwall gave direction to the prayer meeting and shared various items that required God's intervention. He encouraged any one who felt lead to lead in prayer, to take their liberty in the Lord.

There was a tremendous spirit of anticipation as different members of the congregation brought various requests to the Lord in prayer.

At the conclusion of the prayer meeting, a sense of togetherness seemed to permeate the prayer room. There was a unity of faith that was overwhelming. It would appear that each 'prayer warrior' left the meeting with the assurance that God had already answered prayer.

The family returned home without much conversation. In fact, there was hardly any conversation even as they prepared for bed. It was as though they didn't want to distract from the awareness of the Spirit of God experienced during the prayer meeting.

Charley entered his office Thursday morning and started right away to ensure he was prepared for the study that night. Once he had reviewed the material and was assured within himself that he was ready, he set it aside and gave attention to further developments for Eternal Perspective.

Charley was quite pleased with the turnout for this initial meeting. Apart from serving coffee and doughnuts, there was a sense of fellowship in the room as they were seated.

Charley began by introducing himself and giving testimony to God's guidance in bringing him to Glad Tidings, and subsequently to lead this Bible study. He asked those in attendance to bring the development of the study to the Lord in prayer in their private time of devotion. He went on to share his desire that the study would provide an avenue for inviting others and would serve as an opportunity for evangelism.

The study has been identified as: Majestic Perspective, and will focus on the process of rising above the mundane level of relationship with God, to a higher and more magnificent dependency on the Spirit of God, which will result in an overview and outlook that will allow for a sharing in the awesomeness of God that goes beyond anything they have seen or experienced.

As Charley continued to share the thrust of the study, you could sense anticipation gripping the hearts of those who had gathered for this first meeting.

Charley encouraged study from the passage found in II Kings 6:8-17. It is from this portion of Scripture that the study will focus.

Charley concluded the study by reading this portion of Scripture. He then closed the meeting with prayer.

Upon his return home, Sally asked how his first session went. He was pleased that he was able to share with Sally the aura of anticipation that he sensed from those in attendance. He felt it was a good beginning.

He went to David's room to say goodnight as David settled for bed. He then sat with Sally over a cup of coffee before heading for bed.

Charley began his day as he did each day. This being Friday, there was in his mind a different focus as he prepared to drive to meet with the leadership of Eternal Perspective.

Bruce met him in the hall as he was heading to his office and welcomed Charley. As they headed for his office, Bruce informed Charley they would be meeting in the board-room. As Charley entered the broad-room, he was surprised to see such a large gathering. Introductions were given around the table, and Bruce opened the meeting with prayer.

Charley became aware that seated in the room were supervisors from each program that had been established to give support to the under-privileged. Charley was impressed with the size and impact of this ministry.

When discussion from each established program was finished, attention then focused on Charley and how things were developing in his community.

Charley brought them up to date on the fact that he had met with a real estate agent, and that a number of homes would be visited. He also made reference to the ad he had placed in the local newspaper asking for staff. He showed Bruce the ad he had placed in the paper.

He had two requests for help. One was that someone would meet with him and the real estate agent to visit possible residential settings, and the other request was that someone would join him during the interviews for staff.

Bruce was very pleased with both requests. He stated that by Charley making these requests, it highlighted in his mind, the fact that Charley was not taking the position of a lone wolf, but was truly a team player. He went on to state, that he would meet with Charley and the real estate agent. One of the program senior counselors told Charley that he would be willing to join him when conducting interviews. He asked that Charley would give as much advanced notice as possible for the interviews.

Charley told them he would be collecting applications when he returned home. He felt that enough time had passed for there to be a favourable response to his ad. He asked Bruce if there was a preferred day he would be able to meet with him and the real estate agent. Tuesday would work best for Bruce next week. Charley stated he would set up the meeting.

The meeting concluded with each person expressing

appreciation for what God was doing and for His faithfulness and guidance.

The meeting concluded quite early, and this left a good portion of the day for Charley to spend with Sally and David.

On the way home, he thought that maybe he should go past the post office to see if there was any mail, especially responses from the ad. Just as soon as he entertained that thought, a sense of caution settled over him. He had second thoughts of allowing what could be left for another day, to take away from the time he had committed to Sally and David. Charley knew himself pretty well, and he knew that if he collected the mail, that he would be tempted to pull himself aside and go to his office and begin going through each letter. Having had this second thought, he continued driving straight home.

Both Sally and David were glad to see him pull into the driveway. It was as though they were both looking for his return.

There wasn't a whole lot of conversation regarding the meeting. Charley chose to zero in on what plans had been made for the rest of the day. He was reminded that David would be attending the youth meeting that night. David was looking forward to what would be his first night attending the youth meeting.

Sally proceeded to tell Charley that she needed to do some grocery shopping and was waiting for him to come home so she could go. After she left, Charley asked David if he had been doing anything special on his computer. David had been in contact with the company that had shown interest in David's ability in programming. They were working towards setting up a meeting to meet with him and his parents. David was just a little excited (that was certainly an understatement).

Charley asked David how his garden was coming along. There was a little hesitation with David's response. He told his dad that he was going to try and give some attention to the garden on Saturday. It seemed as though the development of his computer programming took precedence.

Charley left David's room, and went outside to see what yard work needed to be done.

It was such a nice day, that maybe it would be a good idea to do the yard work this afternoon. Charley came inside and changed into his gardening clothes.

He returned and brought the lawnmower out from the garage, and fired it up. He was quite involved in cutting the grass, when David appeared on the scene. He asked his dad if he needed any help. Charley responded that the lawn would need to be trimmed. David said he would do that, and headed for the garage to get the trimmer.

This turned out to be a father and son endeavour. This was great!

Sally returned as they were both engaged in their various areas of yard work. She was glad Charley noticed her pulling into the driveway. She was counting on him helping her bring the groceries inside. This was the first 'real' grocery shopping Sally had done since moving. Before this time, she would just pick up odds and ends, but it was now time to stock the shelves.

As Charley came to the car to bring the groceries in, he asked her if there was anything left for the other shoppers. This brought a smile and a comment from Sally. "You guys love to eat don't you"? Charley just smiled as he picked up the bags of groceries.

When he had taken the last bag of groceries in from the car, he left Sally to put the groceries away and returned to the yard.

Just as Charley was heading back to finish the yard

work, the phone rang. The parents of one of the young people who were planning on attending the meeting that night, called to ask if David would like to accompany them to the meeting. Sally stated that she was quite sure David would appreciate meeting one of the young people and going to the meeting with them. If David had made other arrangements, she would call back.

Not long after, they both came inside after finishing their yard work. Sally proceeded to tell David of the call and asked if he had made other arrangements for getting to the meeting. This invitation was great. It would give him a good start towards getting to know the young people. He looked forward to going to the meeting with this family.

The three of them became very busy preparing for supper.

Following the meal, they entered into a time for family devotions. This family time continues to be very important for the three of them. Because they have made it a crucial part of each day, obligations and commitments that have to be addressed in the evening, have not infringed on this family time for devotions. This certainly adds credence to the importance they each placed on this time.

The table was cleared and the kitchen brought back into shape as David hurried to get ready. Charley invited the young fellow inside as he rang the doorbell. He introduced himself and waited for David. David recognized Peter as one of the kids that had made him welcome that first Sunday during the welcome dinner following the service.

They left the house to attend the youth meeting.

Charley prepared a cup of coffee and some tarts were placed on a plate for Sally as he invited her to join him in the living-room. As they were relaxing in the comfort of their home, Sally asked Charley how he was handling everything. He responded that he was experiencing a high level of comfort and inner peace. He continues to reach out for the guidance and support of the Holy Spirit as he works at developing the two areas of ministry. He continued to share with Sally of the high level of anticipation he continues to enjoy. It seems as though he is just a step behind what God is doing. There is no doubt at all, that God is going before him and preparing the way. It isn't that he doesn't have to really concentrate and work at putting material together. He certainly has had to reach back and be creative, but there has not been the struggle where it seemed as though he was going to the well and finding it empty. The reality of being directed to come to this new community, and to Glad Tidings, continues to cause thanksgiving and praise to God.

Sally mentioned that she is so thankful how everything is coming together. When she said that, she paused as though to catch her breathe. She didn't want to express it, but she did wonder how long it would last. Would there come a time when it would not be so smooth. Charley interjected with the truth of God's faithfulness. He is confident that God is in control, and that He can be counted on to be faithful.

Charley reminded Sally of the conversation she had had with Pastor Bailey at which time he had admonished her, to take one day at a time, and focus on that which is lovely. To focus on what is good.

Sally thanked him for reminding her and asked that he would continue to help her to remain positive. Charley reassured Sally that he needed her to stand beside him as well, and he would continue to stand beside her and David.

They each thanked God for the closeness they enjoyed with each other.

The rest of the evening consisted in small talk as they waited for the return of David.

David came into the house very excited with the outcome of the first youth meeting since coming to Glad Tidings. He found the youth pastor, Steve to be a cool guy. He was hoping that good friendships will develop.

The day ended on a positive note.

Charley began his day as usual, but when finishing his time of spiritual attentiveness, he had a brainwave of thought. Sally and David were still in bed. He thought this would be a good time to fix them breakfast. He had perfected a certain level of skill in preparing pancakes, and began to prepare them. It wasn't too long before both Sally and David came to the kitchen and wondered what was going on. Sally remembered what had taken place the last time Charley had prepared breakfast. That was when he was entertaining thoughts of moving. What is he up to now?

Charley thought he should put their minds at ease, and was quick to tell them he had no hidden agenda. He just felt like giving them a special token of love. They were both overcome with emotion.

Charley had thought of asking if they wanted to go for a drive in the country, but he as well remembered what had taken place the last time he asked them to go for a drive. He decided not to go down that road. (Pardon the pun)

He did ask if they had anything they would like to do this being Saturday. Both of them seemed to be taken off guard. This was not a standard thing for Charley to ask. They didn't quite know how to handle this. They both looked at each other as if to say, "What has happened to my dad/my husband?" They both asked if they could have some time to think about it. Charley sensed their reaction, and just smiled to himself.

There was a community event that looked interesting. Charley asked if they would be interested in checking this out. They each thought it would be good, so they agreed to take it in.

It ended up being a country fair. There was a midway and different booths were you could try your skill at knocking objects off shelves, plus a host of other attractions. It was interesting and fun. The cotton candy wasn't too shabby either. They enjoyed themselves.

Saturday ended on relaxed note. There was no heightened activity the rest of the day, and they retired looking forward to attending the Sunday services.

Sunday was a full day attending both services at Glad Tidings. They each took time for their 'Sunday afternoon nap'. Pastor Cornwall shared very inspiring and directive sermons in both services.

Now that the week-end was over, it was time to get back to the challenges of the work week. Charley made his way to the post office on his way to his office, and found quite a large amount of letters in the box. He was sure that many if not all of these letters were in response to the ad. His first task upon entering his office was to open his mail.

He was very pleased with the response, and the number of what appeared to be suitable candidates. After he had opened the letters, he put them aside and attended to another task. The real estate agent was very eager to set time aside to meet with him and Bruce Tuesday afternoon.

The meeting with the ministry team was again very inspirational with various notes of praise and thanksgiving shared. The meditation Pastor Cornwall chose for the meeting was very uplifting. The meeting ended with prayer and again, a sense of unity permeated the room.

Of the three homes they were shown, one seemed to

stand out that required the least renovations to meet the needs of the population they would be serving. This home was secured for future consideration.

Another appointment was arranged for the following week at which time financial arrangements would be discussed.

Charley and Bruce went back to Charley's office.

Now that definite plans were made for a residential setting in that particular neighbourhood, a notice of intent would need to be given to the neighbours. Charley would begin work on that immediately.

Bruce was quite pleased with the amount of letters he saw in response to the ad. This was the first 'batch' of letters that Charley had received. He was quite sure there would be more.

In regards to the hiring and training of staff, Charley thought to share an idea he had been thinking about. With the completion of the interviews, could those who have been hired, work with staff in a number of established homes to receive training and exposure to the thrust of Eternal Perspective? This idea was met with favour and enthusiasm from Bruce, and he would work to arrange that.

He asked Charley if there was anything else he needed to discuss before the meeting on Friday. There was nothing outstanding right now, and he would look forward in seeing him at the meeting on Friday.

When Bruce left, Charley began to open letters.

There were quite a few favourable responses to the opportunity to serve with Eternal Perspective. Charley was anxious to begin the interviewing process.

He set to one side those that were suitable at face value. These he separated from those that could be viewed as questionable.

Charley finished working on questions to be used during the interviews, and went to his car. It was a very involved day.

Following family devotions, Sally prepared to leave for her meeting. That left David and Charley to spend time together. David was eager to show his dad what he had been working on during the day on the computer. Charley continues to be impressed with the skill level of this young man.

When he tried to explain what he had been doing, all Charley could do was give David his attention, but the information seemed to go right over his head.

Charley asked David if he would be interested in having a game of chess. David looked puzzled. He had never played chess. Charley knew this and was leading David 'down the path'. He realized this would be a challenge for David, and was anxious to see how he would handle it.

It wasn't long into the instructions David received, that Charley could see that David was rising to the challenge.

The time David had spent showing his dad what he had been doing on the computer, and the time it took for David to be shown the basic approach to chess, seemed to have flown by. Sally was coming in the door.

The scene witnessed by Sally was very encouraging. Sally, being the type of person she is, did not find it difficult to recall previous areas of concern. As she saw David and Charley engaged in a game of chess, it reinforced appreciation and thanksgiving for the breakthrough in the relationship of David and Charley. She was moved by what she saw.

When the game ended, David went off to his room, and Charley made Sally a cup of coffee and asked her how the meeting went.

It was very interesting in that the group had been meeting for quite a long time, but a decision will be made to change the time of the meeting. It was suggested that it may be beneficial to have the meeting in the morning. Apparently, there are a number of ladies that would like to attend, but due to their family situations, cannot attend in the evening. A decision will be made in the next couple of weeks.

The meeting itself was quite interesting and inspirational. She proceeded to tell Charley that she is very glad to be part of this group.

Wednesday began with a high degree of anticipation for Charley. He wondered how many more letters he would find waiting for him at the post office. He was not surprised to find quite a few letters in the box. He was anxious to examine them.

He treated this group of letters the same way he had dealt with the first batch of letters. There was a fair number of letters that appeared suitable at face value, for an interview.

When he had completed examining this group of letters, he closed the file and proceeded to work on the letter of intent that would be given to the neighbours in the area of the home that had been designated for Eternal Perspective.

It was a letter that would provide a level of comfort for the neighbours. It was intended to put the neighbours at ease as to the type of individuals that would be served in the home. As well as state the purpose and intent of this home, an invitation to meet would also be extended to any neighbour seeking more information. They could contact Charley to arrange a meeting.

After he had finished the letter and prepared it for mailing, he began working on the material for the study.

At the end of the day, he mailed the letters of intent.

The prayer meeting was again very inspiring. This weekly gathering was providing closeness as prayer requests were made and a spirit of anticipation filled the room. It is difficult to fully explain the dynamics of this evening, but suffice to say, it was extremely moving. The drive home was very quiet as they each seemed to revile in what they individually received and were exposed to. It was a meaningful experience for the three of them.

Following a snack, David headed off to bed, while Charley and Sally sat for a time in the living-room before going to bed. There was very little conversation other than appreciation for the reality of the presence of God that was so very evident during the meeting.

Charley was very aware of the large number of new participates that were gathering for the Bible study. With such an influx of new people, he sensed it would be helpful to reintroduce the thrust and focus of the study.

Majestic Perspective is the focus and thrust of the study. The study will serve as an aid in the pilgrimage towards an outlook and view of the majesty and awesomeness of our God, that will lift us higher and beyond a mundane and 'run-of-mill' perspective.

He then opened the study with prayer.

II Kings 6:8-23 provided the initial setting for the study.

Charley began to explore the setting of this portion of Scripture.

He focused largely on the response and reaction of the servant of Elisha to the circumstances facing both he and the prophet.

It could be said that the servant displayed a fearful perspective. Is the servant to be criticized for his response? Charley encouraged input from those in attendance. There were a number of comments that revealed an in depth examination of the setting.

Comments varied from criticism of the servant to expressions of sympathy.

The servant that was serving Elisha in this setting was

a new servant. This was the first recorded experience this servant had since joining with Elisha. It is possible he had heard of how Elisha had been used of God, but he had not seen for himself any occasion of Divine intervention.

You can understand his horror when he went out early in the morning, and saw the city surrounded with horses and chariots. A further description was given as a heavy or a strong host. (II Kings 6:14 N.I.V.)

Is the servant to be criticized for being afraid? What caused him to be afraid? What could the servant have done in this situation?

In order for a correct assessment to be made of the servant's perspective, we must look closely at what he was up against.

The servant saw the entire city surrounded with a strong or heavy host with horses and chariots.

It was not a matter of him casually walking to Elisha and stating in a matter of fact way, "Oh Elisha, when I went out this morning, I noticed there were a number of soldiers with horses and chariots gathered around the city".

This is one of those situations where we can try and put ourselves in the shoes of the servant. He was terrified. He ran back to Elisha and cried out to him. "Elisha, what are we going to do?" He was gripped with fear.

Fear was causing the servant to experience a perspective that was laced with fear. What other option did the servant have? What was there for the servant to draw from that would change or allow him to have a different perspective?

Charley chose to leave this series of questions unanswered. He suggested that each one conduct a study on the effect of fear. There were numerous accounts in Scripture that dealt with fear. Charley asked that those who would be willing, to engage in a study and prepare to share their findings at the study next week.

He then closed the study with prayer.

As he rehearsed the outcome and progress of the study in his mind, he began to recall the struggle he had had before the move to this new community. It suddenly dawned on him the reason he had positioned himself behind that façade, was because of fear. He had to present himself as he did for fear of being rejected, of being looked upon as less than the highly regarded individual he wanted to be. This fear resulted in him having a limited perspective. Wow, what a revelation!

When Charley entered the house, Sally could see how entrenched he was in his thoughts. She hesitated in asking how the study went. Charley took the initiative and began to share the revelation he had received. This insight moved Charley to regard the importance and thrust of developing a Majestic Perspective. The fear that had plagued him prior to his release hindered him from experiencing a Majestic Perspective. He was victimized resulting in a lesser view of God.

He was able to identify to some degree with Elisha's servant.

He shared with Sally his appreciation for the continued 'tone' of the study from the week before.

The anticipation that gripped his heart seemed to make what had been an hour's drive, less than the 60 minutes. He was actually quite anxious to meet with the co-workers of Eternal Perspective.

Everyone is so appreciative of each other. Charley finds this so positive. There seems to be an ongoing level of support without any element of superiority. This is so refreshing.

When time came to 'get down to business' regarding developments with Charley, a wave of anticipation seemed to sweep over the group. When Charley displayed the large amount of responses to his ad, it added to the mood. Bruce will meet with Charley and the real estate agent on Tuesday. Roger (one of the staff members) will meet with Charley on Wednesday to begin the interviewing process. They will in all likelihood need more than just the one day for initial interviews in that there are quite a large number of candidates. It was agreed that interviews would be held from 8:00 a.m. Wednesday morning. Charley has his work cut out for him in setting up these interviews.

There was still a good part of the day left after he arrived home to spend with Sally and David. The time schedule seems to be working well.

Consistency in giving attention to individual responsibilities for the three of them is paying dividends. A routine is developing that is acceptable to each of them. With the routine that is developing, a high sense of accountability is also becoming evident. This accountability is 'there'. There is no need for examination of or a searching for this accountability.

In essence, accountability to each other sets in when Charley arrives home from his meeting on Friday. This accountability continues until he goes back to work on Monday.

Charley wasted no time in setting up interviews. Interviews will run from 8:00 a.m. Wednesday morning with the last interview scheduled for 3:30. Charley found that there were still a good number of applicants that he took at 'face value', for which he had not scheduled an interview. He made the decision to set up interviews for Thursday morning. An appointment was made with the real estate agent for 1:00 Tuesday afternoon.

Roger was very supportive of the schedule for the interviews. He was even supportive of the invitation to stay over in preparation for the interviews that would be conducted Thursday morning.

Bruce was thankful for the afternoon appointment with the real estate agent, and was looking forward to getting this matter settled as it related to the home.

By the time Charley headed for home at the end of the day, he knew he had been working. He was tired.

During their time of family devotions, the whole issue of interviews was brought to the Lord in prayer. When the subject of having Roger stay over was brought up, there was no hesitation in the least from Sally. She expressed pleasure at being able to be of assistance. The sofa in the family room would be more than suitable.

Charley arrived at his office well before the start of the weekly ministry meeting, and prepared his agenda for the day. The meeting itself took basically the same form as the previous meeting with the same degree of support for each other being very evident.

Bruce arrived well before the scheduled time to meet with the real estate agent.

The real estate agent was very pleased with the decision that was made to present an offer on the home designated for the first residence for Eternal Perspective in this new community. Charley was pleased that this major step had finally been taken. What both he and Bruce were hoping and praying for, was that the offer would be accepted.

While they waited for the agent to contact them, they proceeded to discuss financial issues associated with this new location. Everything seemed to be coming together well. There didn't seem to be any area that was causing caution or real concern.

They didn't have to wait too long for the response from the real estate agent. When Charley answered the phone and found it was the agent, he almost had to tell him to slow down. He was so excited to be able to tell Charley that the offer had been accepted and in reality, they had their first home for Eternal Perspective. Talk about a time of thanksgiving and praise to God for His provision. Yes!!

The agent was on his way to finalize everything before Bruce headed back home.

What a day!

As well as preparing a schedule for initial interviews, Charley realized he had another task that couldn't be overlooked. Those applicants not granted an interview had to be contacted. It was at this point Charley recognized the need for office help. He toyed with the idea of asking Sally if she would assist him until such time as he was able to hire someone to work in the office.

She accepted the opportunity to be of help and assistance to Charley with the stipulation that it would be a temporary arrangement. She wanted to be sure that Charley would begin immediately to hire a permanent office worker. He gave her the assurance he would.

Her first major job was to contact those who were not successful in their application to serve with Eternal Perspective. Charley composed the letter and after they were signed, the letters were mailed.

Sally was thankful she was able to get a good start on this task early enough so she could still prepare for her meeting.

Even though time was tight, the priority of having family devotions continued to reign supreme.

Sally left leaving 'the men' to clear the kitchen and get things back to normal in the home.

David was involved in a computer assignment that required his immediate attention. Charley was left alone and he sat and read the evening paper and relaxed.

It wasn't too long before David joined his dad in the living-room.

As he joined his dad, he began to tell him of the meeting the computer people wanted to have. They wanted to meet both parents to discuss the possibility of him becoming more involved in their computer programming. David asked when they could meet. Charley paused for a moment, and told David he would have to discuss this with his mother. It would probably be Friday afternoon before they could meet, but he would have to wait until he had a chance to speak with Sally.

Sally returned to find both of them in conversation in the living-room. Charley thought this may be a good time to discuss when it would be good to meet with these computer people. David began to fill his mother in on the details. She listened, and thought that perhaps Friday evening would be good, or even late Friday afternoon. Charley and David smiled at each other. They were quick to tell Sally that they had thought the same thing, but wanted her to give input.

With that news, David excused himself, and went to his room.

Charley proceeded to ask Sally how the meeting went. It seems as though the possibility of changing the time of the meeting, was not being received as enthusiastically as first thought. In fact when the subject came up during the meeting, a severe degree of tension was felt. Oh my! This was the first 'wrinkle' that had been noticed in what had been a smooth flow of interaction since they had joined Glad Tidings.

Charley asked if there was any resolution. Sally responded with a troubled expression; "No". Charley stated that that was unfortunate.

Sally seemed very troubled by this. Charley tried to reassure her that once again, when God is moving and doing that which is according to His will, and begins to penetrate areas requiring invasion, there will be resistance. He further stated that they need to bring this before the Lord in prayer in their family prayer time.

Not long after, they retired for the night.

Before Charley dropped off to sleep, he wondered if this was an example of self-absorption Pastor Cornwall had made reference to some time ago.

Wednesday started with much planning. Items needing attention began to pile up.

Sally had brought the letters home that she was preparing to mail. She had taken over Charley's home office.

David needed to contact the computer people to set up the meeting.

Charley needed to contact Bruce to determine what homes would be available in which the new staff could be trained. When this information was given to Charley, he would then pass that on to those who were hired.

Roger arrived well before the first interview. This allowed time for prayer and an opportunity to ensure they were both on the same page as it related to the process they would use.

A half hour was set aside for lunch. This was all the time they needed, as they were anxious to get back to the task at hand.

The interviews went well, and they were both grateful for the quality of those being interviewed.

After supper and following their family devotions, Charley asked Sally if she and David would mind if he and Roger stayed behind. Charley thought this would be of benefit in assessing the result of the interviews, and would help prepare them for the interviews scheduled for the morning. Both Sally and David offered their support with Charley and Roger staying behind.

This proved to be a masterful decision in that they were able to determine who should be offered positions with Eternal Perspective.

Sally returned with David and expressed to both Charley and Roger of the continued reality of the presence of God they experienced during the prayer meeting. David told his dad that they had asked prayer regarding the interviewing process, which God would give guidance to those who should be hired.

Roger was shown the sofa in the family room where he was to spend the night. Sally had made the bed ready for Roger. He offered appreciation.

The day started quite early as Roger and Charley headed out the door in order to be at the office well before the first interview.

Once again, they were pleased with the quality of each applicant.

The last interview concluded at 12:00 noon.

Over lunch, decisions were made as to who should be offered positions with Eternal Perspective. Following lunch with decisions being made as to successful applicants, Roger headed for home. Charley expressed his appreciation for the help and assistance he was able to give.

Charley thought it would be in his best interest, to meet with the new staff members even before they went for their training. This would also give him an opportunity to complete the paperwork that was required for new staff.

He reserved one of the banquet halls, and even arranged to have a luncheon for the new members of Eternal Perspective. This was arranged for Monday afternoon.

He was fortunate in that he was able to contact each one who had been successful from the interviews and were now hired as staff for Eternal Perspective.

He was ecstatic in that he was able to get this out of the way so early in the day.

As the day progressed, he began to evaluate the whole range of responsibilities that were 'on his plate'. He realized he was only one man, and not superman at that. It wasn't that he was feeling overwhelmed, but his past work experience taught him the need to be balanced, in the use of time against the task he faced. His plate was full. Was there something he needed to do about it? Was it getting too full?

He determined to keep a close watch on this.

Before leaving for supper, he reviewed the material in preparation for the study. He was looking forward to possible responses from those who accepted the assignment to investigate the effect of fear.

Sally continues to display tremendous ability in the kitchen. It seems as though each supper meal excels the previous meal.

Family devotions centred largely on the study for that night, as well as the situation with the ladies group and the meeting with the computer people scheduled for Friday. As they each entered into this time of reflection, it became quite obvious of how busy and entrenched they were each becoming in various activities.

There was a large attendance at the study. In fact for many, this was their first night.

Charley opened the study with prayer gave a warm welcome for each one in attendance.

He rehearsed the assignment given last week, and asked if anyone had accepted the challenge and would like to share their findings. There was it seemed, a wave of hands that shot up indicating they had something to share. Charley was very impressed and eager to hear what they had prepared.

One after another shared what they considered significant insight into the state of Elisha's servant and the effect fear had on him.

Interestingly enough as Charley listened to each contribution, there was no reference to the insight he had had following the study last week.

He thanked each one for their contribution, and asked that they each turn to the reference in II Kings chapter 6.

Charley then began to read once again the setting in which the servant found himself.

Charley stressed the fact that the servant was gripped with fear. This fear was more than just a shaking in his boots. It was a fear that caused him to be stricken with near-sightedness hindering him from seeing far off.

Charley proceeded to share of how fear can effect how we look at ourselves and our personal situation in life.

He began to describe the situation in which a young man found himself. This man had obtained a position of influence with a particular company, and had developed a work ethic that was well received. He began to place such importance on maintaining the high level of prestige he had reached, that all he could focus on, was how he could maintain that level of importance.

He began to develop a façade that appeared to give him a safe area behind which he could hide. It was discovered that he had a fear of failure. Failure with being regarded consistently as a valued member of the team with which he worked. All he could see was the 'now' behind the façade he had developed. He had a very limited perspective on life and particularly on the input and guidance of the One he served.

Fear of rejection hindered him from possessing a majestic perspective of the grace and influence of the God he served.

You see, this young man had committed his life to Jesus, and was trying to live for Him, but with a very limited perspective.

The façade, behind which he hid, began to affect his relationship with his wife and son. This had to be dealt with.

It was when he accepted his responsibility to be a help-mate to his wife and a father to his son, beyond anything else, was when his vision was enlarged. He began to experience a majestic perspective of the awesomeness and grandeur of the God he served.

This view allowed him to grab hold with bull-dog tenacity to the promises of God and the reality that God who began a good work in him, would carry it on to completion until the day of Christ Jesus. Philippians 1:6 (N.I.V.)

An excitement with expectation gripped his heart as never before. From that point forward, he began to see and experience an invasion of the Spirit of God in ways he had not experienced before. This invasion caused him to rest in the love and presence of the Lord that allowed him to trust that God was able to do exceedingly and abundantly above and beyond all he asked or thought, according to the power that worked in him.

Charley sensed in that room, anticipation to what God was going to do in the lives of those who were willing to reach out to Him in faith.

He did not sense direction to proceed with further investigation of the setting found in the Scripture. He sensed he should conclude the study with an appeal, to allow God to minister to them individually, to reestablish His commitment to take them deeper and higher in His grace and love than they had ever experienced before.

Following this appeal, he closed the study with prayer.

He arrived home with a high degree of thanksgiving for what had transpired at the study. He looked forward in sharing with both Sally and David of how God intervened.

Sally and David were both encouraged as they heard Charley's report of the study.

During the drive for his weekly meeting with Eternal

Perspective, he gave serious thought to share his need for a director to work with him in developing the ministry in his community. The more he thought about this, the more he became convinced that it was time.

When the focus of the meeting centred on Charley, he did not hesitate in the least to share his concern and make his request. Interestingly enough, there was no discussion as to the validity of his request. In fact, unbeknown to Charley, there had already been discussion of the need for a director to be considered for the first home in Charley's community.

This breakthrough took Charley off guard. Surprisingly enough, one of the senior counselors of an established home, had already discussed with Bruce his desire to move.

Roger asked Charley when he would like him to start his role as his first staff member.

Charley was speechless. My lands! God intervened again. Praise His name!

The only response he could come up with was "Tomorrow".

Roger smiled and stated that that would be a problem as he would have to find a place to live, and would have to ensure everything was left in order in the home he was presently working in. Charley was aware that this would be the case, and asked Roger to tell him when he would be able to start working with him. Roger agreed to this, and told Charley he would assess his situation, and get back to him shortly.

The timing of this could not have been better. Charley invited Roger to the gathering scheduled for Monday. As well, Roger could give tremendous guidance to the training of new staff in the established homes. Everything was coming together so well.

Due to the firm hold Charley was displaying in developing the new area of ministry in his community, and the high regard of confidence Bruce had in Charley's leadership, there was no need for Charley to attend a weekly meeting. Charley would be asked to attend monthly meetings effective immediately. Charley thanked Bruce for his vote of confidence.

The meeting concluded with the leadership gathering around Charley and expressing appreciation for the leadership he was giving to the new location, and gave assurance that they would continue praying that God would lead and guide in every aspect of the work in the new community. In fact, Bruce lead in prayer asking for God's continued blessing and guidance. Charley expressed heartfelt appreciation and thanksgiving.

He was anxious to tell Sally and David of the outcome of the meeting.

As Charley was entering the house, David came out of nowhere and reminded him that this was the night for the meeting with the computer people. It was also youth meeting night. What was David to do? Due to the fact that the computer people had requested to meet with his parents seemed to imply there would be more discussion at that level than at his. He didn't think it would be out of line for him to attend the youth meeting.

Due to the time of the meeting with the computer personnel, Sally thought it would be better to have the supper meal earlier. This would also allow them time to have their family devotions before the meeting.

Supper was good, as usual, and they were then able to enter into their time of meditation. Each area requiring God's guidance was brought forward in prayer with expectancy that God would answer prayer.

Following their family devotions, David prepared to leave for the meeting. It wasn't long before there was a knock at the door as Peter escorted David to the car.

The personnel from the computer company expressed appreciation for the level of expertise David had shown. They were very impressed, especially due to how young David is. They wanted to meet with his parents to discuss payment for David's work he had been doing for them. With David being so young, it would be best from a legal standpoint, to have any financial arrangement filtered through his parents. Both Charley and Sally agreed that this would certainly be the route they would want to go. David would be paid for each program he created for clients that requested computer service. A contract would be drawn up with either parent being the channel through which funds would flow. They were both asked if they would support this idea. They both said they would. An amount was discussed and agreed to, with the commitment that a contract would be drawn up and brought to them for signing. A future meeting was planned, and both Charley and Sally expressed appreciation for their willingness to involve David in this undertaking. They were told they must be very proud of David, to which they both beamed with recognition of how blessed they were in having such a fine young man. They shook hands as they left.

It must have been difficult for David to focus on the youth meeting when he knew a meeting was going on regarding computer involvement. As soon as he crashed through the door upon his entrance home, the first question he asked was; "How did the meeting go?" He listened very intently as he was told the outcome. He was very excited.

He was than asked how the youth meeting went. He was very direct in stating he really enjoyed the meeting, and was so glad to be able to take part. There was nothing especially outstanding in regards to the format of the meeting itself, but there was a real sense of togetherness with the kids as they entered into the meeting.

There was a definite distinction in the services on Sunday. Pastor Cornwall delivered the message with a conviction they had not sensed before. The reality of the presence of God overshadowed every aspect of the service. Something was taking place that was causing a stir. It was as though everyone was thinking; "What is going to happen next?"

There was a heightened sense of excitement as each new employee of Eternal Perspective came into the banquet hall. Roger was able to attend and mingled with each new member of the team. Charley hadn't intended this gathering to be a 'formal' meeting, but he did want to place emphasis on the thrust of Eternal Perspective.

He proceeded to share the rationale and how the name clearly describes the focus of Eternal Perspective.

As each individual comes into the care of Eternal Perspective, we need to look beyond the physical needs of that individual, and ask that we be taken beyond the exterior, and regard that person as someone whom the Lord in His wisdom and plan, has brought into our lives. We would begin to see that person as one for whom Christ died and has brought them into our care to help prepare them for eternity. We come along side to help and guide.

He then asked if there were any questions or concerns or any area in which he could be of help.

Roger echoed what Charley shared, and added that he had really appreciated the opportunity he had been given to have served with Eternal Perspective. His role has been more 'hands-on' than what Charley's role and responsibility has and will be, but each one has the same focus.

Directions were given to the home each member will visit beginning tomorrow morning.

The meal was served and more conversation ensued

until it was time to leave

There were many comments of appreciation for the opportunity to have gotten together in that format, to get to know each other, and to be reminded of the thrust of Eternal Perspective.

Roger lingered behind and spoke with Charley. He had been able to tie everything up in the home he had been working, and as soon as he is able to secure an apartment in the new community, he would be able to move. Charley asked if he needed any help in that regard. There were a number of apartments available, and he had planned on looking at few later that day.

Charley invited him for supper before he headed back to his home.

Sally was pleased to be able to offer support to Roger, and welcomed him.

Roger seemed like a nice guy, and had worked with Eternal Perspective just over three years. He had started as a residential counselor, and had been promoted to senior counselor. He found his skill and interest level to be 'hands-on'. Surprisingly enough, he has no desire to become more entrenched in managerial responsibilities. He is quite content where he is. This may change as he gets older and perhaps gets married and has a family, but right now, he is content.

He expressed appreciation for the supper, and prepared to travel back home.

Family devotions took on a most intensive form. As each request was brought forward in prayer, there was a heightened sense of expectation. You might say, faith grabbed hold and they were each raised to a higher level of expectation. This was expressed by the three of them as they brought forward individual areas needing God's intervention.

There is nothing mediocre in any aspect of their lives.

It seems as though the three of them are waiting with baited breathe as to what God is going to do next.

This posture and position is not new to them. It has been their focus before they moved to this new community. What continues to transpire within them is an expectation. They have each come to that reality due to events taking place in their lives that occurred beyond what they themselves were able to do. In other words, "God did it without me."

It is refreshing and inspirational to see a family stand firmly on the promises of God, and literally trust Him for everything. The upside of this is that God can be counted on to do above and beyond anything that has been thought of or experienced.

The three of them - Charley, Sally and David- have had and will have personal struggles when a stand like this is/will be taken, but God is no man's debtor. What He has promised, He is able and willing to perform and carry out.

Charley continues to experience the reality of God's presence and assistance regarding development of Eternal Perspective as well as guidance for the Bible study.

Sally has come to grips concerning the situation with the ladies group. Through prayer, she has come to the point of grabbing herself by the scruff of her neck (spiritually speaking) with the determination to stand tall with the reality that this is God's work, and that He will overrule and His will, will be done. She has reached that point where she will voice her trust in God if so lead during the next group meeting.

Charley has never seen her take such a definitive stand before.

David has addressed the opportunity to immerse himself in developing computer programs with total disregard for his youthfulness. He as well, has come to the realization that God in His wisdom is allowing him to develop this skill for a Divine purpose.

Even though this family has taken a position that is somewhat foreign to the general population, they do not apologize, but seek to be channels through which God can flow to be a blessing.

Roger was able to secure an apartment, and due to the fact that training for the new staff was taking place in established homes, he is able to take time to prepare the physical home in the new community. He and Charley are developing a close work relationship that will prove to be of benefit in days to come.

Developments continue to be very positive in the effort to establish the ministry of Eternal Perspective. An office worker has been hired, and contact has been made to determine who will be served in the new home.

One month has passed since the new staff have been hired and trained. It is now time for them to take their rightful place in the home for which they have been hired.

Excitement filled the atmosphere as the staff began their first day on the job.

Charley presented the work schedule for the first week which included a time of prayer each morning and a weekly meeting each Wednesday.

The first week was very busy with furnishings, painting and everything else that is part of setting up a new home. Roger laid the groundwork as far as appliances coming into the home which was very helpful.

The format of the weekly meeting is to provide opportunity to share concerns and be kept 'up to speed' on future developments. This weekly meeting will hopefully eliminate surprises.

A meeting has been scheduled to meet with those individuals who will be served in the new home. This meeting will take place on Monday.

As much as Charley enjoys working closely with the staff, there continues to be an ongoing sense of there needing to be an actual director working in the home. He can't seem to shake what seems to be a compulsion. He will definitely take this to the Lord in prayer to determine God's will.

He will also share this with Bruce at the next meeting with Eternal Perspective.

Even though there seems to be a leveling off of the high degree of intensity that prevailed earlier, there still continues to be a high level of expectation and a looking forward to what God is going to do. Interestingly, throughout this high level of expectation, there has never been a forsaking of or a denial of responsibilities throughout this entire process. It brings to mind the question Moses was asked in preparation of leading the Israelites out of Egypt. He was asked; "What is that in your hand?" Moses replied, "A rod." He was told to use that rod. The implication being to use what you have.

The Butterworth family has come to accept the fact, that God would have them use what He has given them.

Attention continues to be given to detail with loose ends being tied up.

Individuals requiring support are now coming into the care of Eternal Perspective.

The contract has been signed with the computer service, and David continues to give serious attention to his responsibilities.

Sally took a very uncompromising stand at the ladies group, with the result that she has been asked to consider serving on the executive.

Attendance and enthusiasm continues to increase at the weekly Bible study.

A strong work ethic and procedures are being developed and followed, for which there is continual thanksgiving.

Bruce listened very intently to Charley's plea for a director. There was no hesitation when telling him that he would give attention to meeting this need. Actually, what Bruce will do from his end, is to advertise for the position of director. In that this falls within the managerial level, he will give direction to the initial interview. He would then expect Charley to be included in the second interview. Bruce will initiate this immediately.

Charley was looking forward to his time with Sally and David. On the way home, he did decide to 'drop in' to see how things were going in the residence. He was very pleased with what he saw, and the staff was glad to see him, not to mention the individual's enthusiasm in seeing the man who helped them 'get out of that bad place'. The scene and the input from those being served, was very touching.

Charley left and arrived home with still lots of time to spend with Sally and David. When he shared with Sally the impact of the scene at the residence, there was no element of condemnation for Charley stopping there on his way home. In fact, Sally told him she would have been terribly disappointed if he hadn't dropped in.

Pastor Cornwall extended a warm welcome to the staff and the individuals of Eternal Perspective that were in attendance Sunday morning. When the welcome was given, those being served in the home seemed to beam with appreciation of being made to feel special. What an introduction to the ministry of Eternal Perspective in this new setting.

There continues to be so many positive outcomes to this whole process that it sometimes causes a holding of one's breath seemingly waiting for the 'other shoe to drop'.

Comments have been heard expressing the thought that it is too good to be true.

Pastor Cornwall continues to follow the leading of the Holy Spirit in proclaiming the majesty and awesomeness of God. There has been and continues to be such an overwhelming reality of the presence of God, that you find yourself not wanting to leave the service even when the benediction is pronounced.

The reality experienced on-going in the Sunday services, is being experienced by other groups gathering through the week. It does not matter whether the gathering is in a formal 'religious setting' or otherwise. Those giving leadership are very clear, that as they gather, they are gathering in the name of the Lord, and they stand on the promise that where two or three are gathered in His name, He is in the midst.

It is becoming regular practice for Charley to discuss with both Sally and David, that what they are witnessing and experiencing, is the moving of the Holy Spirit not unlike the former days, of the outpouring of the Holy Spirit. God is moving.

Charley received a phone call from Bruce, inviting him to attend the second interview of two individuals, who have earned the right to a second interview for the position of Director of the residential setting in his community. The interviews are scheduled in the morning beginning at 10:00. Charley thanked him for the call, and stated he is looking forward to the completion of this process with the need being met.

Stanley seemed to have a clearer understanding of the role and responsibilities of a director in a residential setting than Jonathan, and yet Jonathan expressed a stronger dependency on the help and guidance of the Holy Spirit when addressing situations in the home.

Charley wondered if Jonathan would be more pliable and teachable than Stanley. On the other hand, would Jonathan need more guidance in addressing issues that required director skills that Stanley may have already acquired?

Following the second interview, Charley did not reach a conclusion in his mind as to which individual he should hire. Bruce was aware of Charley's dilemma, and suggested that another interview should be given. This was met with quick approval.

They will conduct another interview the same time tomorrow.

Charley will compose questions and scenarios that will address the two areas of concern that was causing trepidation and uncertainty in his mind.

Both individuals were somewhat taken aback when notified of another interview, but they each stated they would attend.

Stanley was very forthright in his understanding of the role of a director in a residential setting. When Charley presented a scenario of a situation arising in the home regarding an individual being served, there was no hesitation as to what decision had to be made. Stanley followed up by stating that the well being of the individual in our care had to be the priority.

When a scenario was presented involving a staff person who was having difficulties in their personal life that was having an effect on their job, Stanley was very quick to offer a solution. "If the staff person was not able to leave their problems at home and come to work and carry out the job effectively, I would meet with them and give them a warning with a time-frame in which to improve, and if no improvement was made, they would be terminated".

Bruce interjected with the question of whether there would be any compassion extended to the staff person.

The answer given was that if he as the Director of the home began to act as a counselor to members of the staff team, this would take time away from carrying out other duties and responsibilities. Stanley went on to say, "There comes a point when maturity has to be reached, and a person has to deal with issues, and get over it".

Both Bruce and Charley tried not to let Stanley see them gaze at each other when Stanley gave this input, but it certainly got their attention.

Charley thanked Stanley for coming, and stated they would get back to him either later today or sometime tomorrow.

The same scenario was given to Jonathan. He admitted there were areas of being a Director that he would have to 'bone up on', but the needs of the individuals in our care would without question, be on the top of the priority list. He would make every effort to become knowledgeable in the responsibilities of a Director, and if he was given the position, they would not regret giving him this opportunity.

When asked regarding the staff member who was having difficulties in their personal life that was having an effect on their job, Jonathan hesitated for a moment, and gave his input.

"Eternal Perspective from what I understand it to be, is a ministry based approach to coming along side those individuals needing support and encouragement. That support has to come from those who have been visited by God and given what they needed. I'm not beginning to preach, but I am reminded of the Scripture that states that the help we received in our time of need, is the same help we are to give to others who are in need. The individuals in our care will respond in a positive way when they see how supportive we are to each other. There has to be accountability, but there has to be a coming along side to offer support as well. I think a Director should be holding each staff person in prayer on an on-going daily basis".

He also interjected that the staff person having personal struggles, would of necessity, be held accountable to perform and carry out the requirements of the job. There would be no hesitation in this regard, but running alongside that accountability, would be support and encouragement.

Neither Charley nor Bruce tried to hide their approval with Jonathan's input. They did however have to be very professional in their response to Jonathan. He was told that they would be getting back to him either later today, or sometime tomorrow.

With that, Jonathan left the office.

Charley looked at Bruce, and Bruce looked back at Charley without any words being spoken. It seemed like forever, before Charley asked, "Should we give him a chance to get home before we call him?" Bruce smiled and said, "I think so".

They were both impressed with the skill level of Stanley, but felt he would have difficulty following the supportive ministry aspect of Eternal Perspective.

Jonathan's skill level may be lower than what they would have wanted, but his verbal commitment to work to enhance and develop managerial skills, was impressive. The fact that he was so very clear in sharing his conviction in holding high the ministry and support aspect of Eternal Perspective, struck a tremendously positive chord in both their hearts.

There was no question that the position of Director for the first home would be offered to Jonathan.

Bruce will contact Stanley, leaving Charley to give the good news to Jonathan with details as far as his moving, etc.

Jonathan expressed appreciation and gratitude for being offered the position. He reiterated to Charley that he
would not be disappointed.

Charley asked when he would be able to start. He
would have to give a two week notice at his present em-
ployment, and would like to secure an apartment for him
and his wife before starting.

Charley asked if three weeks would give him enough
time to take care of this. Jonathan stated he would plan to
start working at Eternal Perspective in three weeks time.

Charley ended the conversation welcoming him to the
team.

Jonathan was welcomed royally by the team. Roger
seemed especially relieved in that he could now assume
the role and responsibilities of a Senior Counselor instead of continuing to be regarded and looked upon as
the Director.

Jonathan made contact with each team member individually as well as making a point to spend time with those
being served. It was a good beginning for Jonathan.

Over the next period of time, he immersed himself in
studies and took advantage of opportunities that would
expose him to what was required as the Director of the
home. From Charley's perspective, Jonathan was making
tremendous headway. The relationship that was developing between he and Jonathan, was certainly of benefit to
the whole team and the individuals in the home.

Roger as well, was proving to be an invaluable asset to
the whole thrust of ministry in the home. There was no
trace or evidence of any ill will towards Jonathan. Even
though Roger was aware of Jonathan's lack of 'director
smarts', he chose to take the high road and offer support
to the new Director. This spoke volumes to the team, and
especially to Charley. He was really impressed with the
attitude Roger displayed towards Jonathan.

The daily operation and level of care in the home continued to go above and beyond anything that had even begun to be imagined. The team was really pulling together, and the support they give each other was quite obvious.

Charley was now able to take the position of overseer in many areas that are developing. In his moments of reflection, his heart continues to overflow with thanksgiving and praise to God for His intervention and help. There is no doubt in his mind, that God is making bare His arm and revealing His power and majesty in every area of his life and in the 'mission field' in which he has been placed.

As he continued to reflect, again, he was overcome with thanksgiving when giving thought to how Sally and David were being used in ways that went above and beyond anything they had thought of.

Sally was elected to serve on the board of the ladies group, and besides giving leadership in this area she became very involved in the home-schooling group in the community.

David continued to excel beyond the expectations of the computer personnel, and his skill level was paying great dividends to the computer service he was working for, as well as to those who tapped into their services. The youth group at the church was experiencing tremendous growth not only numerically, but there was a wave of spiritual vitality that was having an impact in the community.

Pastor Cornwall's leadership is an inspiration to anyone being touched by his ministry. There has been no hesitation in proclaiming the richness of God's grace and mercy. There continues to be a tremendous reality of the presence of God at every service. Emphasis to wait on God permeates each service.

Charley continued to explore the development of the

relationship between Elisha and his servant during the Bible study. The study centered on the effects of fear with the result being that many came forward expressing their gratitude to the exposure and revelation of how debilitating fear can be, and how insidious it is. The study proved to be an 'eye-opener'.

There was now the need to move forward and explore and discover victory over fear. What position did Elisha take when the servant came back from viewing the city surrounded with a strong force?

Charley explored another situation not unlike the situation with Elisha and his servant. King Hezekiah spoke encouragingly to the captains of his army. He told them, "Be strong and courageous, be not afraid nor dismayed for the *enemy* (added) or for the *entire* (added) multitude that is with him: for there be more with us than with him:

II Chronicles 32:7.

King Hezekiah's comment following these words of encouragement seemed to leap off the page.

"With him is an arm of flesh; but with us is the Lord our God to help us and to fight our battles". II Chron.32:8.

This setting ends with the words; the people trusted in the words of the king. Another translation renders this verse; and the people gained confidence from what Hezekiah the king of Judah said. II Chron.32:8 (N.I.V.)

The reality of trusting in the arm of the Lord came forth with thunderous force.

When the eyes of the servant of Elisha were opened, he was able to see beyond his fear and experienced a perspective that went above and beyond his limited perspective. He was introduced to a majestic perspective that raised him to higher heights of expectancy and dependency on the power and awesomeness of God.

Whereas before, the servant was hindered and blinded by a natural and limited perspective that caused him to focus entirely on what was causing him fear. When Elisha prayed that the eyes of the servant would be opened, faith gripped the heart of the servant, and launched him into a realm of expectancy based on the power of God.

The servant was raised above and beyond what he saw and expected from a natural standpoint. From the natural standpoint, the only thing the servant saw was defeat. "We are surrounded by an innumerable army. What are we going to do Elisha? I'm terrified!" Elisha told him that there was a greater number with them, than there was with those who were surrounding the city. He then prayed that the eyes of the servant would be opened. The Scripture states that the eyes of the servant were opened and that he saw the mountain full of horses and chariots of fire surrounding Elisha.

The horses and chariots of fire surrounding Elisha were seen after the eyes of the servant were opened following the prayer of Elisha. As long as the servant remained with a limited perspective and view, he was only able to see the natural armies that surrounded the city. He was able to see the mountain full of horses and chariots of fire through a majestic perspective as a result of Elisha's prayer.

The servant of Elisha moved from the natural realm into the spiritual realm. He was risen above and beyond.

~~~~~~~~~~~~~~~~~

Chapter Five
ABOVE AND BEYOND

MAKING THE drive to meet with Bruce and the managerial team of Eternal Perspective was causing Charley a little concern and a slight hint of anxiety. Why was he summoned to attend this meeting? He had been meeting monthly, and there had never been any indication of concern. These and other thoughts flooded his mind.

The distance he needed to travel gave him time to assess the development of the ministry in his community. Instead of becoming deluged with negative 'what ifs', he began to rejoice within his heart of what God had done, that went above and beyond anything he had thought of. Whatever the outcome and the purpose of this meeting, he has a note of thanksgiving to God for His faithfulness.

As he entered the conference room, he did not pick up on any preparation made for an ambush. In fact, Charley was welcomed with open arms and heartfelt expressions of appreciation. Once again, he had the question come to his mind; "What is going on?"

Bruce welcomed him to the meeting, and asked that everyone bow for a word of prayer. He prayed that God would indeed make His presence known and would give guidance to the meeting.

Following this prayer, Bruce turned to Charley and

stated that he was probably wondering why he was invited to this meeting. Charley nodded in complete agreement.

Bruce then asked Charley to give them a rundown of what has taken place with Eternal Perspective for almost a year and a half.

Charley began to rehearse the blessings that God has poured out on the ministry of Eternal Perspective. He began by stating that the team continues to be very supportive of each other, and have positioned themselves beside those in need of care and reinforcement.

The individuals themselves have made tremendous strides toward independence and acceptance of their personal responsibilities. Through programs and services that have been introduced to them, they have advanced by leaps and bounds.

As well, the family members of the supported individuals have been very appreciative of the approach taken in the home.

Another tremendous note of thanksgiving is for the acceptance of Eternal Perspective in the community and in particular in that neighbourhood.

He reiterated the fact of sending out letters inviting the neighbours to voice any concern or question they may have had, with a home being established in their neighbourhood. To this day, there has been no negative comment received from the neighbours. The neighbours are very cordial whenever the staff and supported individuals are seen in the community. This is certainly another cause for thanksgiving.

For fear of presenting the development of the ministry in his community as utopia, he shared that there have been areas of concern. A case in point, involved a staff person who was having personal problems that began to affect the quality of work when on shift. Once again however, God intervened and gave guidance. The position Jonathan took during his interview in which he emphasized the supportive role he would need to take, came into focus in a substantial way. He and Roger, the Senior Counselor, worked together and came along side this staff person and gave the support that was required. This support and the way the situation was handled, spoke volumes to the other team members.

There is consistency evidenced throughout the home and its ministry.

Charley concluded by stating his appreciation for being part of the ministry of Eternal Perspective in his community.

Bruce thanked Charley for his input, and a round of applause and verbal praise and thanksgiving to God was shared.

Bruce then began to share the purpose of meeting with Charley.

One of the officials from the Ministry of Community Services, had met with Bruce recently, and discussion centred on the need for additional support from Eternal Perspective. Apparently, a facility that housed developmentally challenged individuals was closing ahead of the proposed schedule that had been prepared.

Comments were made as to how positive the development of the new home had been. The official asked if Eternal Perspective would be interested in opening another home. Bruce said he would have to discuss that with his managerial team and that he would get back to him.

Bruce looked straight at Charley, and asked him; "Would you be interested in opening another home?"

Charley stammered and sought for a response. Wow! Another home! He finally found the words, and said; "Yes".

Another round of applause with verbal thanksgiving to God followed Charley's response.

Bruce thanked Charley for his response, and stated he would like to meet with him Monday morning to discuss development.

He then asked each member to stand and gather around Charley as he led in prayer.

The drive home was very thought-provoking. Once again, he could hardly wait to tell Sally and David.

Sally had wondered what the 'called' meeting was all about as well. She had fleeting thoughts that something unpleasant was 'in the air'. Due to past episodes of counseling and a determination not to dwell on the negative, she sought to dismiss these thoughts. Needless to say, she was very glad to hear the car coming into the driveway.

Charley opened the door and not only did he step inside quickly, he almost flew into the house. Sally determined right away that he had something tremendously important to tell her.

After giving her a big hug, he proceeded to tell her that it would be best if she sat down. He asked that David be called into the living-room while he prepared a cup of coffee for them both with a glass of juice for David.

When the three of them were seated in the living-room, Sally asked Charley to hurry and tell them what happened.

When he had finished giving them the account of the meeting with the end result, neither of them knew what to say.

The remainder of the day was filled with questions and suppositions with a high degree of excitement.

Their family devotional time was filled with thanksgiving and praise to God with requests for His continued help and guidance for this new adventure.

Bruce proceeded to ask Charley what he considered to

be the determining factor for the apparent success in the development of Eternal Perspective in his community.

Charley paused momentarily, and began to place importance on the reality and guidance of the Holy Spirit. He continued to stress the fact of consistency that had been and continues to be followed religiously. The mandate and thrust of the ministry of Eternal Perspective, has been followed consistently throughout every aspect of development. The fact that all staff have committed to this reality, has served to enhance this positive outcome.

Over shadowing all aspects of development is the utter dependency on the work of the Holy Spirit to empower and give insight and direction.

The reality that this is the work of God continues to provide stimulus for dependency on Him.

Bruce stated his appreciation not only for the leadership Charley had given in the development of the ministry, but for positioning himself beside the team members.

He further asked if there were any changes he envisioned in further development of the ministry in his community.

Charley was quick to reassure Bruce that he was determined with the help of God, to stay the course.

Following this exchange, they entered into a period of prayer and discussion on the steps they would follow for further development of Eternal Perspective.

Charley was very clear in describing the course of action he would like to take regarding this new challenge. He would like to have a Director hired immediately. This would allow the Director to become entrenched in the development of the home from the very beginning. It would also allow the Director to put his/her 'stamp' on every aspect of the new home right from the beginning as well.

Bruce listened very intently to Charley's presentation, and agreed with him that this was the ideal direction to take. He further stated that he would begin the process immediately.

Bruce called Charley and shared with him a very interesting piece of information. He had received a fair number of responses to the ad he had placed asking for a Director for the new home for the underprivileged, but one response was received with great surprise. Roger had stated very definitely that he was not seeking to become a Director of a program at this particular time in his life. Bruce held in his hand a letter from Roger, asking for an interview.

Charley expressed surprise as well, but felt this could be regarded as very significant. He felt special emphasis should be placed on the interview Roger would be given. Bruce agreed with Charley's perception.

Tony came across as a good candidate for the position even though his work experience had been in retail. During the interview, it became clear that he had developed a good work ethic that would certainly be of benefit when giving leadership in the home.

One of the first questions Roger was asked during his interview was what caused him to change his mind on becoming a Director. The opportunity to stand-in while a Director was being considered for the new home, gave him a different insight on the role and responsibility of a Director. Even though he had served as a Senior Counselor, he did not have to shoulder the full weight of responsibility for the home. If something didn't work, he could just pass it on to the Director. When standing in as the Director of the new home, there was no one to pass it over to. This heightened responsibility got his attention. He thought that maybe it was time for him to become more involved. He realized even though he would be introduced to a different level of responsibility as the Director, there were numerous other aspects he would need to know. Financial accountability would certainly be one area he would have to become versed in. He did share with Bruce and Charley his desire to become the Director of the new home.

Roger's input and his good work performance, got the attention of both Bruce and Charley to the extent that following his interview, they both agreed that he should be given the responsibility of giving leadership in the new home as the Director.

There was however, a wrinkle that had to be ironed out. Tony came across during his interview, as someone who would be an asset to the ministry, but not as a Director at this time.

They both agreed that he should be given the opportunity to apply for other positions that would be offered.

When he was told of the outcome of the interview, even though he was disappointed in that he was not given the position of Director, he expressed appreciation in being given support in applying for other positions.

Roger expressed appreciation with gratefulness in being hired for the position. He was very quick to assure both Charley and Bruce of his dedication and acceptance of the guidance of the Holy Spirit throughout this process.

A meeting was arranged to address issues that required immediate attention.

Charley was very clear in providing guidelines and areas in which Roger would be responsible. Now that a Director was in place, Charley would have upfront and immediate assistance when addressing every aspect in the development of the new home. Roger would be kept abreast of every detail, and would be encouraged to give input. After all, he is the Director of the new home. Speaking of which, contact will need to be made with a real estate agent. A meeting was scheduled.

Prior to the actual meeting taking place, Roger drove through town and assessed as much as he could, homes that were for sale.

Charley was pleased with the initiative Roger took.

The same real estate agent, who assisted with the first home, was the agent offering assistance this time. This provided a level of comfort in that the agent knew the demands of the new home. Charley and Roger accompanied the real estate agent in assessing available homes.

Three homes appeared suitable for future consideration. Charley would invite Bruce to give his input and guidance in this matter of choosing a possible location for the new home. Another appointment was arranged.

Charley suggested a meeting with Jonathan and Roger would be in order to discuss interviewing and hiring of staff for the new home. The three of them would discuss the approach that would be taken to help ensure consistent support and development of the ministry of Eternal Perspective in the community.

Bruce arrived quite early before meeting with the real estate agent. He wanted to discuss with Charley certain aspects of the development of the second home. This home was to address more intense and higher need individuals than the first home. There would not be any danger to the community, but the level of care and support needed by the staff, would involve a more intense level. The groundwork and position of support that is in effect at the first home, has certainly provided a model for the next home.

Bruce continued to suggest that the staff hired for this second home, would find it helpful to spend time in one of the established homes that is geared to the same level of support that will be required in the second home. Charley was very acceptable to this suggestion.

The home that was chosen to meet the individuals with higher needs was in a rural setting within the community. Both Roger and Charley agreed with the suggestion from Bruce. The real estate agent committed to drawing up the papers. Bruce left to return to his office with a good sense of accomplishment.

A meeting was scheduled with Roger and Jonathan to finalize details regarding the hiring of staff. As well as meeting with both directors, Charley began working on the letter of intent that would be sent to the neighbours living in the vicinity of the new home for Eternal Perspective.

It has certainly been a busy week for Charley. Now that everything was 'in motion' regarding the new home, he was looking forward to spending time with Sally and David. It seems as though he has a mountain of information to catch up on, and he is looking forward to 'catching his breath'.

Sure enough, a lot has been going on in the lives of both Sally and David. Sally asked Charley where he wanted them to start. "Let me get a cup of coffee first" was his initial reply.

David began to share just what was taking place with the computer opportunity. More clients had signed up with more programs being developed. He was even toying with the idea of starting an independent service apart from the company he was working with. This would not be in competition, but would be a broader and unrelated approach.

Sally is very active with the home-schooling group, and the ladies group at the church has added another dimension of activity that is stretching her and providing another level of support as she comes along side those needing help and encouragement.

The Butterworth family is involved in so many areas, but amazingly, there has not been any diminishing of their dependency on the Lord. Their family time of meditation continues to be held in high regard and is consistent.

Charley listened with great enthusiasm. When Sally finished sharing, he was overcome with thanksgiving to God, for giving guidance and provision. He was touched as he made reference to the fact that God in His wisdom, had brought them to this new community, and continues to open doors for them to impact lives of those needing someone to come-along-side. The amazing thing is that God Himself has put this together, and as they continue to seek His face and depend on His strength, He continues to come-along-side. God has shown Himself to do above and beyond anything they have thought about or have experienced. The position they each continue to take, is that of asking what is God going to do next? It seems as though they are one step behind. God through His Holy Spirit prepares, and they are each directed to follow what God has prepared. This continues to provide the three of them with an intensity and dependency on the guidance of the Holy Spirit. It would appear they have each determined to follow and develop that which will bring honour and glory to God.

Charley was pleased with the candidates Roger and Jonathan had chosen for a second interview. Roger will now contact each candidate to inform them of the time for their second interview. Charley is looking forward to sharing in this process with Roger.

With the assignment of Roger as the Director of the new home, this has left Jonathan without a Senior Counselor in his home. Charley suggested to Jonathan that he should begin giving thought to filling that position as soon as possible. The stability of the team could be affected if the position of Senior Counselor was left open too long. Jonathan accepted the advice of Charley, and would address this immediately.

The staff began working in one of the established homes to gain first-hand knowledge of the level of support needed in the new home. Roger and Charley visited the facility to meet with those individuals being considered for the new home. The time they spent together, gave them opportunity to get to know each other a little better in this new level of involvement. Yes, Roger had spent time in the

Butterworth's home, but he was not the Director of a new home at that time. They were both appreciative of this time together.

The new team was settling into their new environment well and taking ownership of their new responsibilities. Their dedication to addressing the high needs of those in their care began to be noticed right away. Charley gave a note of thanksgiving to God for evidence that this new team was committed to building a strong relationship with each other.

Jonathan thought to post the need for a Senior Counselor in his home, and wondered if this was the route to take. Charley shared with Jonathan that his situation was a little different in that he had started with a senior counselor already in place. He suggested to Jonathan, that it may be of benefit, to assess the individual qualities of each team member, and for him (Jonathan) to determine who would provide the leadership that would be an extension of the leadership he gave.

There was no doubt of a 'buzz' that occurred in the home that he was looking for a senior counselor. He should definitely make it a matter of prayer, and seek the guidance of the Holy Spirit. This is another opportunity for God to do above and beyond anything they could imagine. Charley reminded Jonathan that God continues to manifest Himself in doing all things well, and this is another occasion where we can expect Him to be faithful.

During the next team meeting, Jonathan was clear in presenting the need for a Senior Counselor. He chose to ask each member of the team, to submit a name of the team member they thought should be considered for this position. There was to be no lobbying or a 'selling' of themselves to each other in order to get the 'vote'. Each member of the team was encouraged to enter into a fervent time of prayer, to seek the guidance of the Holy Spirit for whom

He would have to fill this position. Jonathan was aware of the daunting task he presented to the team, but stressed that this will serve to reinforce the strong team dynamic that has developed in the home. There was a mood of seriousness as the meeting concluded.

The emphasis of support that enveloped every aspect of development from day one continues to permeate every stage of development. Nothing is considered in and of itself without seeking the guidance and direction of the Holy Spirit.

~~~~~~~~~~~~~~~~~~~

Epilogue

I N THIS parable, the Butterworth family presents the epitome of dependency on God. From resolution to the continued and ongoing development in the new community, prayer and seeking God has been the hallmark of the approach taken.

The example they have been has been contagious. Others have been encouraged to pattern their lives after the example set by the Butterworth family.

During development in the new community, there have been times of struggles. Not everything has gone smooth, but because of the foundation of trust and dependency on God with the assurance that He does all things well, defeat has turned to victory.

It is hoped that the position of faith taken by this family, will provide stimulus to encourage a seeking after God in 'the real world'.

You may not be called to leave your community and become involved developing another ministry, but God is not limited to any area of life, but is faithful to His Word. He can be counted on **to do immeasurably more than all we ask or imagine, according to His power that is at work within us.** Ephesians 3:20 (N.I.V.)

~~~~~~~~~~~~~~~~~

About the Author

B OB RECEIVED his theological training at Zion Bible Institute that was located in East Providence Rhode Island. He graduated in 1960.

Following his graduation, he returned to Canada where he has been actively involved in various aspects of ministry within a 'trans-denominational' setting.

Heightened awareness of the need for dependency on the Holy Spirit was the driving force behind the development of this 'parable'.

Application of the interest and guidance of the Holy Spirit in every aspect of life will result in discovery that He is able and willing to do so much more than we can even begin to imagine or think.

Bob has had a door of opportunity opened to him that highlights the reality of God going above and beyond all that he has even imagined or thought of.

To God be the Glory!